ALPHA'S SUN

RENEE ROSE
LEE SAVINO

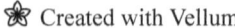 Created with Vellum

WANT FREE BOOKS?

-Go to http://subscribepage.com/alphastemp to sign up for Renee Rose's newsletter and receive a free copy of *Alpha's Temptation, Theirs to Protect, Owned by the Marine, Theirs to Punish, The Alpha's Punishment, Disobedience at the Dressmaker's* and *Her Billionaire Boss*. In addition to the free stories, you will also get special pricing, exclusive previews and news of new releases.

-Go to www.leesavino.com to sign up for Lee Savino's awesomesauce mailing list and get a FREE Berserker book —too hot to publish anywhere else!

PROLOGUE

 *unny*

"You're so hard."

Titus grunts under me. His big body splays out on my massage table, his face hidden, resting on rigid biceps. I've been kneading his shoulders for a half an hour and he hasn't relaxed once. If anything, he's gotten more tense.

I run a hand over the breathtaking expanse of his back, tracing the black vines of his tribal tattoos, scratching lightly. A breath rattles out of him, half growl and half something softer, gentle. A purr.

"You can turn over now," I suggest delicately, and hold up the towel to help him turn with modesty. I never sneak a peek with clients, but with Titus, I can't stop myself. The solid curve of his buttocks, the ridge of his hip, the barest glimpse of something fat and long nestled in a base of wiry hair—

He flops on his back and the source of his tension becomes clear.

"My. You *are* hard." He's either erected a flagpole between his legs under the towel, or he has the most massive erection I've ever seen. He's been lying on that all this time? No wonder he's uncomfortable.

I lick my lips, staring at the tented towel. I should start rubbing his legs—kneading the powerful thighs, working my palm into the ridge above his knee, but there's no point. Not with that marvelous cock saluting the sky. He won't relax until someone takes the edge off his arousal.

That someone is me. *Hurrah!*

I pull a stretchy bracelet off my wrist and tie back my hair. I've already removed my boho shawl, baring my arms and freckled cleavage in my spaghetti-strapped top.

"Let me make you more comfortable," I murmur and reach under the skimpy towel. Sweet goddess above, he is a handful. I grip the pulsing base with one hand and whip off the covering with the other. His flared crown is leaking and I swipe my tongue to taste him—

A fierce growl and Titus knifes up, catching my chin. "You do this for all your clients?" His normally gray eyes blaze bright, bright blue, clashing with the orange and red in the corona around his head.

His aura really is amazing. The passion, the heat—flames crackling with heat—so intense—

"Sunny!"

I blink. He's talking to me. Asking me something. Something important… because the red means—

"You're angry," I breathe, awed by the shimmering sunset colors.

He growls again but his hand on my jaw is gentle. He's so big and powerful, he could break me without a thought. He doesn't, though. He's infinitely gentle, wincing when my table creaks under his massive, muscular bulk. He spent the whole afternoon under my bus, banging wrenches and snarling curses until the motor purred like a kitten. The massage was meant to be a thank-you. I knew we had chemistry… but I never realized how much.

"Answer me," he orders. So bossy. "Do you give all your clients blowjobs?"

I color a little. I believe in free love, but if another man said what he's implying, I'd slap him. Instead, I raise a brow. "Do you get erect whenever you get a massage?"

His chest rises and falls, his breath blowing back the loose tendrils of hair around my face. In a minute he's going to blow. So much anger. I'm not frightened by it. No. What would that amount of passion be like in bed?

"No," he snarls.

I cross my arms over my chest to show him I won't be bullied. His eyes drop to my breasts, soft and clearly outlined under my light tank top.

Titus gives me a look so wild and desperate I take pity on him. "I don't give my clients blowjobs. Not even ones who help me when my bus breaks down." *Or protect me when some bad shit is going down with my daughter.* I touch his rigid thigh and the giant muscle jumps under my small hand. "This is for you, Titus. Only for you."

The light around his head flares bright gold.

"Mine," he rumbles in a voice so deep, I barely make out the word. Before I can protest, he's on me. His giant

3

hand slides under my tank top, over my flat stomach to cup my loose breast.

"No bra. I knew it."

"I never wear bras," I inform him. "Or panties."

He makes a helpless noise and drops to his knees on the floor. His large hands flip up my flowy skirt before he leans in, presses his face to my bare pussy and inhales. *Oh my goddess.* I lean back on the table, my legs too weak to hold me up.

"Titus—"

"Quiet." His left hand, still under my tank, squeezes my breast hard. "I've had just about enough of you prancing around, flaunting your tight little bod—fuck!" The fingers of his right hand glide into my sopping pussy. "How are you so tight?"

"Yoga," I gasp. "Lots of yoga."

"I mean here," he rumbles, finger-fucking me. "Pussy squeezing me like it's gonna snap off my fingers. Fuck!"

"Ah, oh… that? It's been awhile—" How long has it been since I've gotten laid? I'm totally sex-positive, but I've hit a dry spell. "There's been a lot going on. The mafia, my daughter in trouble—"

"Shut up," he murmurs against my pussy, not unkindly. "This is how it's gonna go down. I'm going to eat you until you scream. Then I'm going to fuck you 'til you scream some more."

He licks up my slit and my knees buckle. "Titus," I sigh.

"That's right, baby. Say my name. I'm the one fucking you. No one else."

Ah, so delightfully possessive. I would laugh but

there's an edge to his words. The tightness in his jaw speaks of pain. Someone hurt this big, beautiful man.

I settle my hand on his jaw. "Tonight, I'm yours."

With a growl bordering on a roar, he picks me up and strides to the bedroom, kicking the door.

THREE DAYS LATER...

THE SOFT LIGHT of day falls across my face. I slither out from underneath Titus' giant tattooed arm and slip off the bed without waking him. His face is more relaxed than it's been this whole week. Since the attempted massage, we've barely left bed, only leaving to visit a barbecue with Titus' son Tank and their motorcycle club. For a biker, Titus is pretty uptight, but now he's sleeping like the dead.

Good sex will do that to a man. I mentally buff my nails on my shirt. I did that.

I tiptoe to my bag, wincing as the bed creaks. It's sagging on one side—broken. *Oops.* I slap a hand over my mouth before I giggle like a girl. Titus is uptight and controlling as they come, but when he lets loose? The bed isn't the only thing feeling the force of his passion. I'm going to be sore for days, but I don't mind. It was magnificent sex. Unbridled, wild, rough. I think Titus even scared himself with how badly he wanted me. How much he needed to claim me.

So hot.

But all good things must come to an end.

I pull out one of my hand-painted cards—a watercolor of Cathedral Rock up in Sedona—and flip it over. On the back I use a black calligraphy pen to write:

Titus,

Thank you for everything.

I gnaw on my lower lip, remembering the pain that crossed his face. A woman hurt Titus, and I might be a pacifist but I'd claw the bitch's eyes out if I met her. But it's not my fight.

I tap the pen against the card. What to write? *Wish you were ready for a relationship? Call me when you figure your shit out?*

Instead, I pen:

I hope we'll meet again soon.

Love,

Sunny.

There. Short and sweet. It says everything I have to say to him. I creep out of the apartment the motorcycle club provided for me this past week and shut the door gently. I'll ask my daughter to pick up my massage table and store it for me until I return to Tucson. She put down roots and found her soulmate here. She's safe now, living with Titus' son. Foxfire and Tank were meant to be.

Titus and me… that's another story. I don't know what our future holds, but leaving is the right thing to do.

Titus and I have chemistry—lots of it. But I'm way too much for the guy.

Story of my life.

Titus is like his spirit animal—the wolf. He's meant to roam free. He's a hunter, but once he caught me, he didn't know what to do with me.

And I'll be damned if I stick around where I'm just going to get hurt again.

If we're meant to be, the Universe will throw us back together again.

I'm sure of that.

I tiptoe down the sidewalk like a college girl doing the walk of shame out of the frat house and climb in Daisy, my VW bus. It starts right up, thanks to Titus.

The road blurs as I drive away, but I don't look back.

I can't.

Leaving is the right thing to do, no matter how much it hurts.

I PARK my motorcycle at the Rio Grande gorge bridge and walk down to check out the scene at the end of the bridge.

And it is a scene. There are vendors assembled on the side, some with tables set up, some operating out of buses or the backs of pickup trucks. There are pinon nuts for sale. Local honey. Jewelry. The vendors are a mix of Native Americans and hippies.

A bridge stretches across the Rio Grande gorge, a nauseating six hundred or more feet above the giant canyon. I hear a tour guide telling someone it's one of the highest bridges in the country. I recognize it from *Easy Rider* and one of the *Terminator* movies—favorites of mine.

I scent the air, catching the smell of coffee, ice cream,

sweat. The sun beats harder in the high altitude and my leather riding jacket suddenly feels too hot.

I peel it off and toss it over the seat of the bike. I don't know why, but I have a good feeling about this rest area. Like I'm going to get the information I need from one of these humans milling about here. There's a positive energy crackling in the air.

Someone knows something. I'm here for a reason; I can feel it.

My alpha sent me to follow up on some intel we received about another Data X lab out in the high mesa of New Mexico. I scouted around Sandia National Labs, because we thought it might be there, but I caught no scent of shifters. I checked out Roswell, because of the alien lore, but struck out there, too. There may be aliens, but I didn't smell any shifters.

I only know one wolf in New Mexico and he's a loner. No pack, totally off the grid. So off the grid, he doesn't have a phone—landline or cell. It's been years since I've seen him. Hell, I don't even know if he's still around, but I figure if any of the weird shit that went down with the Data-X guys—any government testing on shifters or disappearances happened in his state, he'd know.

So I've come up to the one place I know he always goes in summer—the Taos and Red River area for fishing.

"Titus? Oh my goddess!" A female voice stops me in my tracks and my entire body reacts like a flash flood of lust dumping into my veins.

Fuck.

Not her.

I'm so not up for this right now.

I rotate slowly, and even though I'm prepared to see the brightness that is Sunny Hines, her beauty knocks my knees out from under me.

I flex my jaw, forcing myself to breathe.

"Sunny." It comes out like a growl. Like an admonishment, which I guess it is.

This woman is fucking trouble with a capital Fuck.

A free-loving hippie who blew through my life two years ago like a fucking hurricane. Definitely left damage in her wake. And I hadn't even realized I had anything on the line with her.

She's dressed in a tank top that shows off her slender, muscular arms and her long blonde hair is woven in a braid that hangs across one delicate shoulder. She hurls herself at me.

You wouldn't think a woman so tiny could make such an impact, but I have to brace to catch her full weight, and there's no choice but to pick her up off her feet with a bear hug. Her arms wind around my neck in a stranglehold.

"Sweet goddess above. I knew I'd see you again! It's so great. Such a surprise." She barely breathes between sentences. "How are things? Have you been to Tucson to see the kids?"

I try to extricate myself from the hug, mainly because the feel of those soft, bra-less breasts rubbing over my chest is too much. Especially when combined with her unique scent. I don't know what it is—probably some frankincense or patchouli shit, but on her, it doesn't smell bad. On her, it comes off as feminine power mingled with mysticism.

It smells like danger.

My wolf doesn't think so. My wolf thinks she smells like hedonistic pleasure.

And he's totally down with that.

But I'm not.

Fuck, no. This female—this *human* female—is the last person I need to get involved with. If I think I made a mistake with my first mate, I know without question this one is a hundred times worse.

At least Barbara stuck around a few years to see Titus Junior grow into a little boy. But maybe that's not fair. From what I can tell, Sunny was a great single parent for Foxfire, my son's mate.

But she's ditzy as hell. Like whacko airy-fairy.

I clear my throat trying to step back, but she follows into my personal space. Damn her. "Uh, yeah. I saw the kids a few weeks ago. All good."

"Any talk of grandchildren?" The hope in her face is so blinding I want to look away. People shouldn't show their emotions so clearly. It's unnerving. Does something squirmy to my gut.

"No," I say too gruffly. "At least not that I heard. But I don't go pushing that kind of thing." I glower at her like it's entirely inappropriate for a woman in her fifties—a woman who looks too fucking glorious to be in her fifties —to want grandchildren.

Her expression dims slightly and she pulls back.

I'm instantly sorry for being such a dick. My wolf stirs, restlessly, like he needs me to fix it. ASAP. Before I know what I'm doing, I reach out to touch her arm.

I fucking *stroke* her arm—like I have any right to touch her that way. To caress her sun-kissed soft skin.

"I'm sure they'll come eventually. The kids are still young."

Some kind of pain flits across her face, something I can't decipher, but she nods and turns the smile back up. "Well, what are you doing here, Titus? Clearly you didn't come to see me."

The idea that I would come to see her is ludicrous, and she must know it because a blush creeps up her neck. It may be adorable to see a woman our age blush, but again —the woman's got to stop showing every single emotion. It's fucking dangerous to show so much vulnerability. Especially a woman like her, living alone in that goddamn Airstream. Any guy could take advantage of her. Mow her down.

And that thought leaves my skin prickly with anger.

"I'm on official pack—I mean club business." I'm not sure if Sunny fully understands what we are. She lives in a different dimension. To her, everyone has a spirit animal, which she can see with her inner eye. So she sees mine as a wolf. She saw her daughter's as a fox, so she named her Foxfire. But does she really get that we're shifters? That part is unclear.

If she were a different kind of human, telling her probably would've been necessary. But she sort of accepts it all like it's nothing. I don't think she's actually seen a shifter in their true animal form. Tank swore to his alpha she hadn't, anyway. I don't believe she knows it is a real thing, not a spirit animal.

She came to my son's pack run, the one where I lit up the sky with fireworks to welcome her daughter to the pack, but since she's not a member, I took her on a ride on my motorcycle when the time came for everyone to shift and run.

She stares at me now, open-faced, expecting more.

"It's private business," I add. I'm sure as hell not going to discuss serious pack shit with her.

"Oh. Well great. Do you have a place to stay?"

I look around for her Airstream, but I don't see it. I do see her painted VW bus parked at the edge of the gorge. Daisy, I think she calls it. Insert eye roll. How in the hell did I miss it before? I worked on that thing for a full week, not wanting her risking a breakdown driving around in the ancient pile of screws and bolts.

I don't have a plan for where to sleep yet, but fate knows I'd never fit in the Airstream, if that's where she still sleeps. Not that I plan to get anywhere near her and a bed again, anyway. "I'll figure something out," I say.

Her smile takes another dive.

My wolf fucking hates it.

"Yeah, sure. Great. Well, if you want to grab a beer or something while you're—"

"I don't think so," I cut her off. I need to get away from this female before she snares me in her feminine web again. I still remember how gutted I felt when she left last time. "But thanks."

"Sunny!" A good-looking but clearly weak and inferior human male calls out from a table nearby. "You teaching rooftop yoga tonight?"

Oh, no he didn't.

I seriously think the asshole is challenging me. He may not even understand his own behavior—humans are idiots about pack order dynamics even though they engage in them every day—but I guaran-fucking-tee he saw me talking to Sunny and his nature prompted him to insert himself.

Asshole.

Sunny turns her bright face in his direction. "You know it! Are you coming?"

"Of course. I'm looking forward to opening my hips with you under the sunset."

Sunny snorts, which only partially mollifies my wolf. Really I'd like to go over there and punch the guy right in his gut. Teach him to fucking sniff around my territory.

Whoa.

Pull back, Titus.

This woman is definitely not my territory. I haven't marked her, nor do I plan to. The last time I mated a female it ended badly. Lost me my position in the pack and ruined my kid's life.

But I'm incapable of walking away and letting this guy open his fucking hips with Sunny tonight.

"What's rooftop yoga?" I snarl.

Amusement flickers over Sunny's face. "I teach sunset yoga on the roof of one of the cantinas on the plaza. Why? You going to come?" She folds her arms across her chest with a teasing challenge in her gaze.

And my wolf never backs down from a challenge.

Never, ever.

I splutter as I try to answer. "Yeah." The syllable wobbles across my lips. "What time?"

"Seven o'clock." Her eyes still dance with amusement. "You probably don't have any clothes you can stretch in, though."

Is she giving me an out?

I glance over at fuck-face. "I'll figure something out."

"Well, great." There's false cheerfulness in her voice now, and I don't particularly like it. Does she not want me there? Does she actually want to have a yoga date with fuck-face? She takes a couple steps back from me. "I'll see you there, then."

"Wait—where exactly?"

"On the rooftop patio above La Cantina. Follow the crowd with yoga mats—you can't miss it."

Yoga mats… fuck.

As if she reads my mind, she says, "I'll bring a mat for you." She tosses a wink before she saunters away, the swish of her hips imprinting on my brain like a hypnotic cue for lust.

Oh hell. What did I just do?

I'm out here on pack business, and I'm letting myself get distracted by a female. There's a pattern here that's uncanny. Females are trouble for me. I was kicked out of my pack over a woman. Tank and I wandered around like beggars until Emmett Green took me into his pack in Wolf Ridge, Arizona, north of Phoenix. And now after five minutes with a pretty human, I'm ready to ignore my orders for the most out of character activity on the planet —rooftop yoga.

I must be out of my fucking mind.

$\sim$

SUNNY

. . .

OH LORDY.

I forgot how attractive Titus is. Huge, masculine, muscular goodness. Immovable as a wall, both physically and emotionally.

But he's an alpha male, so when Chas asked about yoga, he couldn't stop himself from throwing his dick in the ring. Yeah, mixed metaphor. My specialty.

How emotionally immature.

And slightly flattering.

Well, it might have been flattering if he hadn't pretty much given me the brush off. So now it's just annoying. Like he doesn't want me, but no one else is allowed to have me either? I don't think so.

I'm not playing that game, big boy.

I'm not playing any game with you. If you want me, come and get it. But if you're still not ready, don't waste my time. I have a life to live.

I head back to my tables and start packing things up for the evening. I haven't sold a single piece today. Which is how it goes. The day felt kinda flat when I woke up this morning, but I still have to get out there and try. I'm fine— money always appears when I need it. The Universe has my back, for sure.

I don't give into the *woe-is-me, I'm a starving artist* thing, because I know that can turn into an identity and it's not one I'm going to choose. I climb behind the wheel of my bus and start her up. She still runs like a dream thanks to the prickly man I just walked away from.

I look around for where he's parked and spot him saddled up on his motorcycle, staring right at me. I lift my hand with an overly-cheerful wave which he doesn't acknowledge. Instead, he guns the motorcycle and takes off with a roar.

Testosterone.

The guy seriously has way too much of it.

He is definitely not a sensitive new age guy. More like King Kong meets caveman.

And yet I still sense he could be the one. There's something in me that feels so vibrant when I'm with him. Like he could be my soulmate. Twin flame. Divine partner.

But he's got his head stuck so far up his ass he wouldn't know his soulmate if she danced naked in front of him. He's the *bros before hos* type all the way.

He has blinders on to almost anything except his precious motorcycle club. And he may be big and strong and fierce, but what he doesn't know is that sometimes vulnerability takes the most courage. Putting yourself out there. Risking your heart. Your emotions. Your very soul for love.

But I'm not anyone to emulate. I've been hurt way too many times. I'm not going to open the door for Titus to walk through unless I know for sure this time he's ready. That it will work.

So yeah, I guess I'm as big of a chicken shit as he is.

I drive to the plaza and park in the lot, then pull the drapes across the bus windows to change into my yoga clothes.

Rooftop yoga is the highlight of my week. Especially now that it's summer and we don't need the heaters anymore. I grab mats and start walking to the plaza, waving to my friends and students also converging.

Taos is a great community—a blend of three diverse

cultures: descendants of the original Spanish settlers who still speak Spanish and hold all the government positions, the Native Americans, who own most of the land in the area, and the hippies who arrived in the sixties and opened the bohemian shops.

I love it, but I don't feel like I'll settle here forever. I'm holding my breath for grandchildren. If Foxfire gets pregnant, I'll move back to Arizona in a heartbeat.

I walk up the stairs to the rooftop where Tara, the cantina owner, is testing the sound equipment.

"Hi, girl, how's it going?" She holds out her hand for my phone, which she connects to the PA. She thought I was crazy when I pitched my idea for sunset yoga up on her rooftop patio last year, but now that she's seen it bring in a large crowd who stay for food and drink specials after, she bends over backwards to accommodate me.

"It's good, totally good."

She squints at me. "Yeah? You don't seem like your usual floaty self."

I force a laugh and rub my lips together. "There's a guy coming tonight."

"Ooh." She waggles her brows. "Which one?"

Yeah, Taos is that small. The joke is that once you've dated every guy on the list of eligible bachelors, you have no choice but to reboot and start again from the top.

I shake my head. "A guy from Arizona. We hooked up once, but... he doesn't like women much."

She purses her lips. "Sounds like a loser to me. Maybe skip this one."

Something tightens in my middle. Almost like I'm offended on his behalf. Titus is not a loser. He's a beautiful

19

and flawed human being, like all of us. I have total acceptance of who he is. I just have to listen to my intuition to
decide if it's in my best interest to get involved with him.

Tara cocks her head. "Aw, you do really like him, don't
you? Well, is he around? I want to meet him."

"He is supposedly coming to yoga, although I can't
imagine how he'll manage. He's built like a semi-truck and
is about as flexible."

She lets out a laugh. "So that's how you like them. I
wouldn't have guessed that. Would've pegged you for
more of the scrawny yoga types. But then, we go for opposites, don't we?"

I shake my head. "I'm not going for this one," I say,
like I've already made up my mind.

Some sliver of hope in the center of my chest withers
when the words leave my mouth, though.

"Uh huh." She hands me my phone, which is now
amplified to play my world beat playlist. I take the headset
from her and put it on, testing the mic.

The community is filing in. Chas arrives and sets up
his mat right in front. After that stupid display at the gorge,
I can't even look at him.

The patio fills with at least twenty-five people. I get
the full range of ages and abilities. I'm not egotistical
enough to believe they come for me or my teaching—they
love the atmosphere. The rooftop. The sunset. The music
and the laidback but still genuine class format. There are
young and old, mother-teen combos, super buff river raft
guides, other yogis, and the conglomerate of friendly
faces.

I wave to my friends, Adele, the chocolatier; Charlie,

our postmistress; and Sadie, a kindergarten teacher as they roll their mats out in their habitual places.

I place my hands in front of my heart and bow. "Welcome, everyone. Namaste. Please sit in half lotus on your mat, if that's comfortable." I draw in a breath to give them my short suggestion for meditation tonight. I had a plan to talk about being in allowance of others, but it no longer feels relevant.

"Yoga is a practice with rhythm. There's a timing with breath and movement. You know when to move, when to hold, when to release, when to recover. So is life. Paying attention to timing makes all the difference. Don't push when something's not ready. Don't hesitate when something's ripe. This week, as you move through life, ask the question—is the timing right for this? Should I bide my time or should I pounce? When is time to release the old? When is time to bring in the new?"

I go quiet, allowing them a moment of silence to reflect on that.

"Close your eyes." I wait for them to comply. "We'll begin with three oms. Please release your breath. And after the inhale, we begin." I make the tone as Titus' huge form appears at the top of the stairs.

He's wearing a navy blue t-shirt that molds to his ripped muscles and a pair of sweat-shorts. He looks about as out of place and uncomfortable as a nun in a strip club, so I nod through my om and point to the mat I rolled out for him on the end of the front row.

His brows lower, but he lumbers to the spot and—hilarious—attempts to sit cross-legged. The poor man's lower back and hips are way too tight to allow his knees to open or his spine to straighten. I'd have a little more sympathy if he wasn't looking at me like I'm bat-shit crazy.

I know that look. I've been getting it my whole life.

And Taos—particularly this class—is a place I can be myself. So fuck him.

We finish the three oms.

"And now come to stand at the front of your mat in Tadasana, or mountain pose."

Titus' forehead furrows as he struggles to stand up. I avert my gaze for fear of wounding his pride too much.

"We'll start with our sun salutations. Inhale arms up. And exhale forward fold. Fingertips on the floor or hands on the shins and inhale, lift your head, lift your gaze. Exhale release your head. Take your weight in your hands and step or jump back to plank on the inhale. Exhale push back to downward facing dog."

Poor Titus. It was so mean of me to tempt him into coming. I walk around to where he's struggling to fold his hips toward the sky. "That's it," I murmur, although my voice is amplified so everyone hears it. I place the heel of my hand on his sacrum and apply gentle pressure, encouraging his pelvis to tilt so his sit bones roll up.

He gives a sharp exhale.

"Tread through your feet, bending one knee and the other to stretch your calves."

I slip my hands around the front of his pelvis, thumbs on his back to show him a little more.

I swear I hear a low growl come from his throat. It's not threatening, but my body responds automatically. I pull my hands away and step back.

Okay, buddy. You're on your own.

~

Titus

THIS WOMAN IS FUCKING KILLING me.

I mean, seriously. I might die. Not just the stretching part, although that sucks. I'm a wolf, though. Indestructible. It may hurt now, but I'll recover in twenty minutes. No, it's the fucking cock tease.

I have little Miss Yogi wrapping those heaven-scented hands around my hips—so close to my dick—and there's only one thing running through my mind.

Pound. Her. Hard.

I have an urgent need to get the woman on her knees and show her the best use for that stretchy lithe body.

And the worst thing is every time she walks anywhere near me, guiding us with that sing-song voice of hers, I get a half-boner, which is really fucking hard to hide in these gym shorts.

This is pure agony. It was absolute idiocy that spurred me into coming. Except that dickless prick from the gorge is front and center, trying to show off his prowess. So yeah. I'm not leaving. And I'm a fucking wolf. My body should do anything, even if I am over fifty. I may never have moved this way in my entire life, but I'm damn well going to. Because I'm not going to be out-stretched by pretty-boy over there.

"It's not necessary to push," Sunny intones in that

musical voice of hers. Of course, she's talking to me. "Yoga is not about efforting. It's about acceptance. Know your limits. Know where your body is today, not where you want it to be. Honor your body. Follow your own knowing."

Oh for fuck's sake. I want to shut the female up. With my cock stuffed down her throat.

Okay, that's crude and disrespectful. My wolf is getting far too rowdy. *Down boy.* You don't get to fuck her. We're not going down that path again. Females are a distraction which I clearly can't handle, considering I'm up here pushing my ass to the sky instead of following the trail I was ordered to follow.

And she's not even a wolf.

I'm so pathetic it's scary.

She directs the group into some crazy arm balance—peacock pose. This I can do. I have ab and arm strength in spades. I press my elbows under my ribs, flatten my palms to the mat and extend my legs behind me, hovering parallel to the mat.

The people around me notice and murmur approvingly.

Eat that shit, pretty-boy.

"Yoga is a personal practice. There's no need to compare yourself with others. There's no competition."

She'd look pretty with a gag. A bright pink one to match all the colors she likes to wear. She'd look lovely tied up, too. Naked, of course. Wrists in another bright color, bound to my headboard. I'd leave her feet free, though, so she can show me just how wide those legs spread. Just how bendy she can get with my hands on her.

Oh thank fuck. The class is finally over. At least I think

it is. We're lying on our backs with our eyes closed doing nothing. Corpse pose, I think she called it.

Oh, now the crazy female is walking around rubbing oil on each person's neck and pulling their head away from their shoulders.

My wolf starts growling. He does *not* like her touching every fucker in this class.

When she gets to me, the exotic scent of the oil both calms and excites me. Intoxicates. Or is it her scent? No, it has to be the oil. It's not like a human could tempt a shifter.

Except I know that's a lie.

In my day, it was forbidden to even mix with humans. Definitely forbidden to mate with them. But it seems things are changing. My alpha's son took a human for a mate, and several of his pack members have followed suit.

But I still don't see how that works. A wolf wouldn't get the instinct to mark a human for a mate. It's biologically off. Their offspring may not even be capable of shifting. Why would an animal pick a permanent mate so clearly inferior?

Her small, but deft fingers stroke along the taut muscles of my neck and a low rumble comes out of my chest before I can check it. Almost like a purr, as if I'm a goddamn cat shifter.

She touches between my brows, and I instantly drop into a meditative state. My mind goes quiet. Deep.

I want to ruminate on how that's possible, but thoughts seem unimportant. The slow beat of the music rocks through my body and my heartbeat syncs to it. I feel tingly. Alive. Connected.

It's not a familiar feeling and yet it's like coming home. I know this space.

I don't know how long it goes on. There is no time. Five minutes? An hour?

From a huge distance away, Sunny's voice filters into my head with the gentle suggestion that I roll to my side.

Push up to sit.

My body obeys without my mind engaging in thought. I blink my eyes open and find myself sitting on my mat, facing Sunny's exotic figure. I'm entranced by the chain of butterflies tattooed around her upper arm.

She says some bullshit closing stuff and leads the class through another om and the whole time I just sit and watch her. Trying to figure out what about this human is so damn intriguing to me.

So intriguing she's dangerous. She's going to pull me off my mission—that's something I just can't allow. I resolve to get my ass up off the mat and get the hell out of there, but Sunny's musical voice becomes another invitation.

"Thank you all for joining us tonight. La Cantina has food and drink specials for you all, so if you'd like to stick around and socialize, I'd love to have you. Namaste."

Oh, fuck no.

Of course pretty boy is going to stick around. That's why he's so into rooftop yoga. He gets to watch Sunny in her yoga pants *and* stay for drinks with her. It's like a fucking date to him.

Sure enough, the guy wears a huge smile as he tucks his rolled up mat under his arm and goes to stand beside her.

I skip the rolling the mat part and crumple it in my fist as I stalk over.

Sunny turns her attention to me, but it's with disapproval. "Thanks, Titus," she says drily, taking the mat from my clenched fist.

I growl a low warning in pretty boy's direction.

He responds by moving closer to Sunny. "Ready for a drink?"

To my satisfaction, she inches away. "I'll be there in a bit." She turns her bright face in my direction. "Titus, are you joining us?"

Pretty boy deflates.

My wolf loves it. And my plans to walk away disintegrate. "Yeah. Okay." My voice sounds rusty. I clear it. "Sounds good."

She tugs her hair out of the ponytail that was high on one side of her head and lets her long blonde hair cascade down over her shoulders. "Then let's go."

 *unny*

I DON'T KNOW what possessed me to invite Titus for cocktails. This isn't his crowd. Definitely isn't his scene. But I guess I'm not willing to say goodbye yet. Not when being near him lights my whole body up like a Christmas pole. I mean tree.

I take his hand and lead him into the restaurant. I don't know why I grabbed his hand—maybe to send a message to Chas, whose attention is getting way too annoying. Maybe it's to send a message to Titus that I'm still interested.

Either way, it's too intimate of a gesture. The air between us charges. He chokes on a breath. My nipples go taut.

Chas looks back and takes it in, expression falling.

Titus growls like a wild beast.

It's Animal Kingdom weird and hot as hell.

I slide into the giant circular booth seat where Adele, Charlie, Sadie, Chas and a few other random yogis are gathered and scoot over to make room for Titus.

He frowns, like he's not sure how he got here. Or why he even followed me.

That always seems to be his reaction to me, though. Like he can't stand me but at the same time, he's too attracted to me to leave. I think he might be pissed over the way I left, too. I'm definitely catching remonstrance. Along with a whole six-pack of judgment.

But I'm used to that. I've been too much for men—for most people—my whole life.

That's what I like about Taos. Crazy is the norm here. I fit right in.

"Class was great today, Sunny." Sadie, the little kinder-garten teacher, beams at me.

"Yeah, it was great," Charlie echoes. "I felt a little lightheaded towards the end, but that's because I'm on an all-liquid diet." The waitress sets down water for all of us, and places a tall brew in front of Charlie. The post-mistress must have ordered at the bar as soon as she got here.

"So you're drinking beer?" Adele arches a brow. Charlie gulps her drink and licks her lips. Sadie's eyes widen.

"No, it's cider." Charlie sets the glass down with a thump. "Don't give me that look. It's practically fruit."

Adele shakes her head, looking poised and put-together as always. Even after class, her glossy brown curls are perfect. She turns to Titus. "Hi, I'm Adele, I don't think we've met." My friend leans across the table and offers her hand to Titus.

He surges up like he wants to stand, bumps the table and sloshes the pitcher of ice water our server left.

I don't usually get jealous or insecure, but an unpleasant tug squeezes my solar plexus. My girlfriends are so much younger and cuter than I am. Sadie is Foxfire's age and here I am with gray mixing into the blonde of my hair, making it appear lighter than it really is.

"This is Titus, my son-in-law's father," I explain as everyone starts offering their name and hand to him.

"Are you up here to visit Sunny?" Sadie asks, her dimples making her appear even younger. She is the town's most favorite teacher, and it's easy to see why. Sweet and beautiful and seemingly innocent, she's almost too perfect. Every parent tries to get their kindergartener in her classroom. I hear the principal made a strict "no request rule" after parents were resorting to camping out in her office trying to convince her.

Titus shifts uncomfortably in his seat. "Actually, I didn't know she was up here. We ran into each other today at the gorge bridge."

Sadie turns her smile up a watt. "Lucky you," she breathes.

I almost snort. I doubt Titus shares that sentiment.

Our server appears and I order a margarita and nachos. Titus gets enchiladas and a burrito, despite the server's warning that the burrito is huge.

"Oh, I'm sure he'll put it all down," I pipe in, remembering how much the guy eats. I guess when you're that big, your metabolism runs like crazy.

31

Charlie toasts him with her cider. "Titus, have you taken yoga before?" Of all my girlfriends, she's the most boyish, with a pixie haircut and curvy form hidden under a *Namaste, Motherfucka* t-shirt. She's ripped the collar off so when she leans forward, a hint of her impressive cleavage flashes.

That niggle of jealousy rises up again.

"First and last time," he rumbles.

Everyone laughs and Titus looks down at me. "No offense, sunshine."

I think we're both surprised that the endearment rolled off his tongue so naturally.

Although it's not that big a stretch. My name is Sunny, after all. It's not a new nickname for me. Somehow it's different coming from his lips, though.

He seems uncomfortable, like he wishes everyone would stop talking to him, so I redirect. "Charlie, how's post office business?"

She shrugs. "Same-o, same-o. Someone had crickets delivered to their PO box, though, and they chirped all freaking day long. Drove us all nuts."

"Oh, crickets. I should get some to show my students. They'd love it." Sadie tilts her head to the side, looking adorable as she thinks.

"Won't Scott just love that," Charlie teases.

Sadie's gaze drops to the table.

"Sadie?" Adele picks up on it right away. "Are you okay? Did something happen with Scott?"

"We decided to see other people," Sadie says softly.

"Oh no," Charlie growls. "That fathead. Did he cheat on you?"

"That's not what she said," Adele protests, but pain flashes over Sadie's face. "Oh no, he didn't." Adele switches to momma bear mode. "I will end him."

"It's okay," Sadie whispers and Charlie wraps an arm around her.

"Damn straight it'll be okay, after we rip his head off. Men suck." She turns to Titus. "Present company excluded, of course." I notice she doesn't look at Chas.

"Don't ever date in this town," Adele advises Titus who looks like he wants to race for the hills. "It's a fishbowl."

"Drink this," Charlie pushes her cider towards Sadie, whom I've never seen drink anything stronger than a Coke. "It'll put hair on your chest."

"I don't want hair on my chest," Sadie squeaks, but she drinks.

"I never saw you with him. He was so"—Adele makes a face—"fake. The opposite of you, sweetheart."

"Opposites attach," I put in. "Oops, I mean attack. No, *attract*." I pat my lips to apologize for the word jumble. I'm always flubbing up expressions. It's a special gift of mine.

"You're so right. My ex is totally weird. Totally blunt, no tact. Completely opposite to me," Charlie announces. "Anyway, Sadie, I know what you need. A one night fuck!"

Sadie chokes on cider.

Titus pinches the bridge of his nose. He did not expect to get in the middle of girl talk.

"Headache?" I murmur.

"Yeah."

I look with my inner eyes at his auric field and see the giant gray cloud hanging over his head.

"Permission to clear your energy?"

"Come again?"

I hate this part. I have gifts but you can't go messing with people's energy without their permission, and to get permission, I have to explain something they probably won't understand or believe in.

"Just say yes."

His gray eyes are thoughtful, but he nods his head. "Okay."

I imagine a giant vacuum over his head and suck away the gray cloud, keeping at it until every trace is gone. Then I infuse his aura with a soft pink-purple light. "There. Better?"

He frowns and touches his temple. "Uh, yeah. Actually. It's gone."

"Good." I turn back to the conversation at the table and join back in, ignoring the scrutiny I sense from Titus and sucking my margarita down faster than I should.

I can't stop thinking about what will happen next. Will he stick around? Walk me to the bus? Or invite me to his place? Or is he going to say goodbye and good riddance? My intuition does me no good in this situation, which I think relates to his indecision. Like he hasn't made up his own mind.

And I can't decide what I want, either.

That's not true, I definitely want to get physical with Titus.

Tonight.

But I get too fluttery when he's around. Too excited.

And I'm attached to an outcome here, which is always bad. That outcome is not him driving off on that Harley after a *wham, bam, thank you, ma'am.*

I excuse myself to go to the bathroom, climbing over Titus to get out of the booth.

Big mistake.

I lose my footing—or did he pull me down? I land on his lap and... *hello, big guy.*

Definitely happy to see me. Big as I remembered.

"Fates," Titus curses, his breath hitting the back of my ear, his growl awakening every part of me that wasn't already on high sexual alert.

He has one hand on my hip and he pulls me tighter against his lap at the same time he rolls his hips to show me his reaction.

But then, just as quickly, he lifts me. No, he practically throws me off.

The guy is hella strong. I mean, who can deadlift a woman while sitting?

I get catapulted to the floor outside the booth so fast I stumble. My pussy's wet from the encounter—so wet I'm afraid it will show through my yoga pants. I take off to the bathroom as fast as I can.

When I get back, I find cash on the table where Titus had sat.

Even though I knew it was coming, I'm unprepared for the sinkhole of disappointment that drops me three stories in a single second.

Titus

WHAT AM I DOING?

What in the fuck am I doing?

I find myself circling Sunny's VW bus in the parking lot across the street from the plaza. I meant to march out here, get on my bike and drive off.

It was a solid plan.

Okay, fuck that. It was a cowardly plan. Sunny had taken off for the bathroom, and I had a boner as big as the Sears building, and I couldn't get my wolf under control.

So I bailed.

But now I can't bring myself to actually leave. Which seriously pisses me off.

Damn that ridiculous and beautiful human.

The thought of hurting Sunny's feelings shouldn't be such a big factor here, but it is.

Well, she is my daughter-in-law's mother. She's like family. I wouldn't want to give offense and piss off Tank or Foxfire.

Or Sunny.

Yeah, it's totally about Sunny.

There's something magical and mystical, and fuck, yes —*weird*—about the woman.

And that doesn't bother my wolf a bit.

So I'm out here like a stalker, deciding if I should stay or go. And yeah, the Clash song is playing in my head. I had a thing for punk back in high school. Mohawk and everything.

I catch her scent, and I know it's too late.

For some reason that pisses me off even more. I spin around and park my arms across my chest and my ass against her VW bus, which makes the whole thing groan with my weight.

"Titus." She sounds surprised.

And looks hurt.

Fuck.

I don't even know what to say to her. I don't know what I want from her. From this.

So I just stand there, glaring. Growling.

She stops. "You're mad. Why are you mad?"

My nostrils flare at her frankincense and orange scent and my cock gets hard as stone. My wolf is on the edge now. So much I can't think straight.

"Not mad," I growl. My boner throbs under the thin gym shorts.

She tips her head to the side. It's an animal-like gesture —similar to the way she looked before she asked my permission to clear the headache. Like she's using her senses beyond the normal human capacity.

Her eyes widen and then her gaze drops to my swollen cock. "Oh."

Christ.

And that's it. My wolf has had enough.

Before I can stop myself, my hand shoots out to grasp her nape, and I spin her around until her ass hits the bus. I flatten her against it, my mouth colliding with hers.

"Fuck," I rumble against her lips, right before my tongue sweeps into her mouth.

Her lips part, she sucks my tongue, kisses me back.

Her hands brace against my shoulders, but she's not pushing me away, she's pulling me in.

"Get in that fucking bus," I snarl, my humanity gone. "That pussy's mine tonight."

She fumbles with the door, seemingly as desperate as I am. I smack her ass.

Smack it again, hard.

"Ow, Titus." There's laughter in her voice, which is a relief because I'm incapable of dialing back my sexual aggression right now. I need to get between this woman's legs like it's my holy quest.

"That's for being such a fucking cock-tease." I wrap an arm around her waist and pull her soft ass back against the bulge in my shorts. My other hand cups her mons in the front. Her pussy's so wet I can feel the dampness through her yoga pants.

Her knees buckle, and the keys drop to the pavement.

"Titus!" Her voice is shaky. "I can't concentrate when you do that."

I stoop to pick up the keys and get the door open myself. And then I throw her inside. There's a mattress in the back, same as I remember from before. I slam the door shut and push her down on it.

I fall over her and yank her tank top down her shoulders to expose one breast.

My mouth connects with the stiffened peak, sucking it into my mouth, scraping my teeth over it. I give it a slap, and she gasps.

Something about Sunny has me showing all manner of dominance, and she's not even a she-wolf.

Fortunately, she doesn't seem to mind.

Her scent tells me it turns her on.

Her scent.

Fuck, her scent.

I grab the waistband of the yoga pants and tug them down and off. No panties. Damn! I need to taste that nectar she produced for me. Need it on my tongue *now.*

I lick into her, one long slow stroke. The groan that comes from my lips is half-feral. I go in for more, lapping, licking, flicking. I want to please her as badly as I need release. I'm dying to hear her come. To take her over the edge and satisfy her.

I grip her thighs and spread her wider, applying my tongue with more intensity, reveling in the way she squirms and wriggles, the cries and moans that fill the bus. I keep at it until she tears at my hair, inner thighs fighting to close around my head. Then I penetrate her with two fingers and find her G-spot.

Cover her mouth with one hand when she comes.

"Titus," she pants when I uncover it. "Oh my goddess. What are you doing to me?"

"What am *I* doing to *you*?" I rise up onto my knees and shove down the gym shorts to free my cock. "Do you know what you did to me all night long?"

Her lips quirk and I realize she did know. She tortured me on purpose.

I shake my head. "Naughty hu—woman. Very naughty."

I flip her over and slap her pale ass. The sound fills the bus, echoing around the interior. It's a satisfying crack. I smack her again on the other side this time. My handprint blooms red on the first side.

Beautiful.

She wriggles her butt like she's asking for more.

So I give it to her. Five firm slaps—enough to make her gasp and squirm.

Then I hold her down by the nape. "You want it from behind, beautiful?"

"Yes." Her voice is breathy and sweet and there's no hesitation.

And that's when I realize. No condom. I don't carry one because I'm not that kind of guy who goes around picking up random women. Besides, wolves don't get STDs. But she doesn't know that.

"Sunny." My voice sounds strangled. "I don't have a condom. I'm clean, though, I swear. Do you trust me?"

She looks over her shoulder at me. When she hesitates, I seriously think I might implode. But then she nods. "I trust you."

Thank fuck.

"Good girl," I say. The words surprise me. It's not a phrase I've used before. My previous mate didn't inspire this level of dominance or protectiveness.

Strange, since she was a wolf and Sunny isn't.

"Shirt off," I order. And once she's ripped the tank off, I add, "Spread those legs for me, baby. You've got a hard fucking coming now."

She lets out a strangled laugh and spreads her thighs wider. I've never seen anything so goddamn beautiful in my life. She has more butterflies tattooed at the base of her spine, spreading across her hips and then ascending on a diagonal to the shoulder tattoo. I remember the tattoos from last time, but they strike me anew.

"So pretty. Got any new ink, baby?"

"Mmm, you'll have to find out for yourself," she murmurs against the sheets.

Challenge. Accepted.

I nudge her thighs wider and kneel between them, then rub the head of my cock against her entrance. She's still leaking honey, sweet and silky. I slide right in.

"Fuck that's good, baby." I ease back, then slam in hard, causing her to give a little scream.

"Oh, you didn't think I'd be gentle with you, did you?" I repeat the action, loving the way my loins slap up against her ass like another spanking.

She laughs. "I seem to recall you broke a wall last time."

Damn. She's right. She does something crazy to me.

I palm one shoulder to keep her in place, then fuck her with powerful thrusts. I want in deeper, harder.

I know it's too much. I'm sure I'm hurting her—she's human, after all—but I can't seem to stop myself.

All I can do is try to soothe her with my words. "You're taking it like a good girl, though, aren't you, sunshine?"

I fuck so hard the bus bounces on its wheels. Everything in it rattles and shakes.

Sunny's breathing in gasps that I force out of her with each slam in.

She bumps her head against the door and readjusts, pulling her hips up so she's on her knees. I hold tight around her waist and keep pumping hard.

"You like that angle, baby? Where I get in so deep?"

"Yes," she gasps. "Fuck, yes."

Her enthusiasm is too much for me.

"I was thinking about this all through yoga," I confess. "All through dinner."

"Me too!" She's breathless, her face turned to one side against the mattress, hair a wild halo.

"Yeah? Is that why you were such a cock tease?" I slap her flank. "Sitting on my lap and making me hard?"

"You *pulled* me to your lap!" she protests.

Maybe I did. She's probably right. I didn't mean to, but then she was climbing over me, her soft body right over my lap. What was I supposed to do?

"You needed this fuck." I accuse her, even though I'm the one who needed it.

"Yes," she agrees. "Definitely."

And that's when coherent speech becomes impossible. I'm too dizzy with lust, too high on her enthusiastic reception.

I pound and pound until my vision goes to white lightning, and I roar so loud the bus shivers.

And then I come.

I fill her with my cum, soak the sheets. And only when my vision clears and I can breathe again, do I realize she's coming too. Her pussy's squeezing every last drop out of me in quick pulses.

I lower us to the mattress and wrap an arm around her waist, keeping her ass tucked against my lap, my cock still inside her. Our chests move together as we catch our breaths.

My wolf wants to issue all kinds of claims and demands. *Get rid of that pretty boy asshole. You'd better not be touching other men in yoga. This pussy is mine.*

But for once, I'm smart enough to stop myself. I have no claim on Sunny, nor do I intend to claim her.

She can—and will—do whatever the hell she wants, including slipping me a note and driving off the moment I fall asleep.

I already know how this thing between us works.

So this time I do the leaving.

I kiss her neck. "Thank you, Sunny," I murmur. I slip out of her and climb up.

She rolls over. "That's it?" There's accusation in her tone, although I don't know what she wants from me. She's not exactly the settle down and have a relationship type. I'm unable to think of a response because as I rise up, I get the full view of her naked, and my body stills. I can only stare. Drink her magnificence in.

She blinks those blue eyes at me, watching steadily. "Am I going to see you again?"

I clear my throat. Try to make my lips move. "Uh, I'm not sure." I rub the back of my neck.

She drops her face into the sheets. "Right."

I don't know where she gets off being upset. Still, a stab of guilt hits me square in the chest. I did just barge my way into her bus and fuck the daylights out of her.

"Well, I'd like to see you again, Titus."

"Yeah. Yeah, okay. But I gotta go now. I'll come find you." I back out of the bus and shut the door.

I left my motorcycle on the opposite end of the plaza, so I walk back the way I came, through the now empty town square. I'm almost to the other side when I hear the scream of metal on metal and my whole world flips on end.

CHAPTER 3

itus

I NEARLY SHIFT RIGHT THERE in the street.

Somehow, I know the crash involved Sunny. I sprint at top speed to the intersection as a wrecked silver Volvo tears off down a side street.

And there, in the middle of the intersection, is Sunny's bus, smashed on the side like she got T-boned, and spun around facing the sidewalk.

"Sunny!" I shout, leaping over the wall separating me from the road and nearly tearing her door off its hinges.

There's no airbag, nothing soft for her delicate human face to hit. Sunny's forehead rests on the steering wheel and the smell of her blood makes my vision dome. I'm ready to shift to defend her, but there's no one left to fight. The assholes took off after smashing into my lovely human.

"Sunny. Fuck, Sunny." I want to tear the bus apart to make space for her crumpled body. I draw in a deep breath to calm the fuck down.

Christ, she's just a human. A delicate, breakable human.

And such a slender, frail one at that.

I caused this. I left her limp and dazed. She was in no condition to drive—although this accident clearly wasn't her fault. Still, she might have been more aware of her surroundings if she hadn't just been fucked out of her mind.

To my relief, Sunny groans and lifts her head.

"*Sunny*. Don't move, baby. I'll call an ambulance."

"No, no." She attempts to unbuckle her seatbelt and sucks in a sharp breath. Her arm is hanging at a funny angle. She reaches with the other arm. "I'm all right."

Total liar.

She slides out of the bus.

Before her feet can hit the ground, I scoop her straight into my arms. "You're clearly not." Her arm's broken, a large egg has already formed on her forehead and the laceration across her neck and shoulder from the seatbelt makes me want to howl.

Sirens sound close by. A cop car pulls up with the lights spinning.

"Put me down," she mutters.

"No fucking way. I need to get you to a hospital."

"Titus, I'm *fine*. Put me down."

"What happened?" One of the cops demands as his partner calls for an ambulance.

"She got T-boned by a silver Volvo," I tell them. "It took off down that side street there."

"You get a license number?"

I shake my head. I'd been too focused on getting to Sunny to memorize it. "It was a New Mexico plate. I think it had a J and an 8 in it, but I don't remember the rest."

"Were you in the vehicle when the accident happened?"

"No, I heard the crash from the plaza and came running."

The guy eyes Sunny's perch in my arms dubiously. "You never move a victim. Always wait for emergency services. She could have a broken neck, and moving her could leave her paralyzed."

Jesus.

My stomach drops to my shoes.

"I don't have a broken neck," Sunny insists, but she holds up the wrecked arm. "Just a broken arm. And he's putting me down right now. Aren't you, Titus?"

It's only because she sounds out of breath and in pain that I comply. Fuck, maybe she has broken ribs and I'm hurting her more. I gently tip her to her feet and keep a solid arm around her waist to support her. She leans into me, trembling like a flower.

The ambulance arrives and the EMTs take over. Sunny tries to argue about not going in an ambulance, but I cut across her protests. "Don't listen to her. She's going with you, end of story."

Apparently they agree because they get her down on a gurney and put her in the back of the ambulance. "I'll follow in the bus, baby. Everything's gonna be all right."

47

She blinks at me with that cat-like gaze of hers. I see no fear. No angst. Only uncanny assessment.

It should reassure me that she's unafraid, but it doesn't. The female's so out-of-this-world, she might not even realize how hurt she is. She might not recognize when she needs help. I'm sure as shit she wouldn't ask for it. She strikes me as the type who's been taking care of herself her whole life.

Crazy, dangerous woman.

I go to the bus, which is blocking traffic, and am relieved to find it still runs. The bent metal isn't restricting the movement of the tires or engine.

Heart still in my throat, I follow the ambulance to Holy Cross Hospital and head into the waiting area to call my son.

"Hey, Dad." Tank's deep rumble comes through the earpiece. Another surge of guilt ripples through me.

I stab my fingers through my hair. "Hey, uh I called to tell you something. There's been an accident."

"What?" I hear a crunch and I know my son just cracked his phone. He's always had trouble managing his strength.

"It's Foxfire's mom. Sunny's bus was hit by a car. They took her to the hospital for an eval."

"Sunny?" I hear the shocked disbelief in Tank's voice and then Foxfire's frightened one comes on the line.

"What happened to my mom?"

"She was in a car accident but she walked away. I mean, she was on her feet before they put her in the ambulance. Her arm was definitely broken, though."

"Oh my goddess. Are you in Taos with her?"

"Yes. Don't worry, Foxfire. I'll take care of her." The words come out before I can stop them, but I know they're true. As much as it kills me, the mission from my alpha just slid to second priority.

Sunny's hurt and I'm partly responsible. Even if I wasn't, there's no way I'd walk away from her. She's fragile as glass and doesn't even have the advantage of youth to help her rebound from this. She may be laid up for days—even weeks.

And she's utterly alone up here. No pack—family— whatever humans call it. Who knows how reliable these friends of hers are?

"Thanks, Titus. I'm glad you were there." Foxfire's voice sounds shaky. After a pause, she says, "Why are you there?"

"I'm on pack business." I rub my forehead.

Or I'm supposed to be.

Why are humans so damn fragile?

"Do I need to come up there? When are you leaving? How badly is she hurt?"

"Okay, slow down, rainbow," I say, referring to the color—or rather, colors—of her hair. "I don't have answers for you yet. I'll let you know after she's been seen by the doctors."

Foxfire sighs. "Okay. Okay, thanks. Really. I appreciate you being there, Titus. I know you'll take good care of my mom."

Something uncomfortable shifts in my chest. Now I have two females depending on me. Not a good place for me to be.

I mutter my acknowledgement and promise to call

back when I know more. Then I take up a position pacing the hallways of the small hospital.

SUNNY

I'M TRAPPED in a room with a giant wolf-man and no hope of escape.

Seriously, it's that bad.

Titus insisted on bringing me to the little cottage he airbnb'ed. My car is parked out front, but I haven't been allowed to see the damage. It was too dark when we got here last night, and Titus won't let me out of bed today.

He's standing in the bedroom doorway now, doing his best to intimidate me into climbing back under the covers.

Unfortunately, I find his form of intimidation lethally attractive.

"The doctor said I'm fine," I insist. Just some lacerations and bruising. A stiff neck from whiplash. And the broken arm. Which still throbs, even inside the cast.

"I'm gonna call bullshit on that one. Get back in bed before I put you there."

Despite my aches and pains, my pulse picks up at the threat. I don't mind the idea of Titus manhandling me a little. He may be a rough lover, but I enjoyed every second of it.

But the sting of how quickly he took off after sex yesterday is still too fresh. This guy's heart is still marked unavailable.

Too bad he's so damn attractive. Fresh from the shower, he's walking around with his shirt off, without any care about what the sight of his washboard abs is doing to me. I swear, my hormones are stronger in my fifties than they ever were in the years when I was trying to start a family. Nature's sick irony, I guess.

I haven't felt this attracted to a man since Johnny, Foxfire's dad, and even then, I wasn't this horned up.

But there's a similar energy. The wild animal type of man. Johnny's was more furtive, he had a wild spirit he tried to hide. Titus is right out there with his. Riding the Harley, sporting the leather jacket.

"You don't have to to this, Titus." My stomach swoops a little, because if I'm honest, I don't want him to stop. I don't want him to let me leave. But I also don't want him to be here out of guilt or obligation, and I know that's what this is.

Titus walks forward until his ribs hit my breasts. I think he expected me to back up, but when I don't, he reaches down and scoops my ass up under his forearm, lifting me to straddle his waist.

"Titus." I go breathless. My heartbeat taps at the surface, right against his bare skin.

"I told you to stay in that bed," he grumbles. "You're gonna stay there, even if I have to tie you to the headboard."

Sweet goddess above, he didn't just say that.

He's infinitely gentle as he settles me on the bed and when he steps back and examines me, I see genuine concern on his features.

I indulge in the warmth that floods my chest for just a

moment. "Thanks, Titus." I grab his hand and squeeze it. "This is really sweet of you."

He brushes my hair back from my bruised forehead, frowning at the bump. "You got that wrong. I'm not sweet. I'm just doing what anyone would do."

Oh.

Right.

And just like that, the warmth evaporates. It must show on my face, because he takes a step back and pushes his hand through his salt and pepper hair.

He opens his mouth, then closes it again. "You hungry? I can go pick up some donuts or something across the way." He points toward the main drag.

"I'm gluten free," I inform him, knowing he's going to roll his eyes.

He does.

"There's an easy solution," I taunt. "You can let me go. I have food in my RV and I'll be fine on my own."

"No, no. You're not going anywhere. And stop making this so fucking hard." He pins me with a stern glower that makes my pussy clench. "I have shit to do in Taos, but I can't get it done if I'm worried you're going to jump in your bus and run off the second I walk out."

I blink at him.

He leans over me, planting a huge fist on either side of the mattress beside me. "So here's how it's going to go. You're going to tell me what you want for breakfast, and I'm going to get it. Then you're going to curl up on this bed or on the couch out there and rest while I take care of business. And when I get back, you'll be right where I left you. Or there will be consequences. Understand?"

A laugh escapes my lips. I don't know why I love this bossy side of him, but I do. "We'll see."

He growls. It's a real animal growl. A wolf growl.

I get totally wet and my muscles go slack, like my body's just surrendering itself up to him.

His nostrils flare and a ripple of shock runs across his face right before his eyes change from gray to a clearer light blue.

I go from propped up on the bed to flat on my back in a flash, Titus straddling my waist and pinning my good wrist beside my head. "You like trouble, don't you, lady?"

I push against his chest with the casted arm. "Don't call me *lady*."

He leans down and nips my neck, his beard tickling the side of my face. "You don't like that, huh?"

"No." All the pain in my head and arm are forgotten as I roll my hips beneath him.

"What do you like, sunshine?" His voice is gravelly. He moves down and bites my shoulder. His cock settles between my legs, right where I need it, and I lift my hips to rub over it.

"I-I don't know. *Sunshine* is nice."

"Okay, tell me what it's going to take, sunshine. You need a threat of punishment, or a promise of reward? What's going to keep you here?"

I pretty much melt into a puddle at that.

I lick my lips. "Um… both?"

He nods and lifts his torso. He unbuckles his belt and draws it slowly out of the loops.

Tingles run across my skin. I forget to breathe.

He captures my good arm and loops the leather around

the wrist, pulling it taut. I'm suddenly his prisoner when he attaches it to the headboard. "You're gonna stay here while I get breakfast. Now what do you want?"

I sulk. "I want to go with you."

"Nope. You need rest. Tell me."

I consider him for a moment. Think about where we are on the main drag and what's nearby. "Huevos rancheros. Green chile, corn tortillas. You can get them at the diner right across the main drag there."

He nods, apparently satisfied and all business. "I'll be back in a few. Don't move."

I tug on the bound wrist. I'm sure if I wanted to, I could extricate myself, but it would take some work and the use of the fingers on my broken arm, which I don't feel much like jostling.

"Be a good girl, and I'll think about a reward." His gaze drops to my beaded nips and I squirm.

"It had better be a good one," I throw back at him, and he lets out a pained laugh.

"We'll see." He's giving off that angry vibe again, which I think means he's sexually frustrated. Actually, I think it's more complicated than that. He wants me but doesn't want to want me.

I know the feeling, buddy.

He casts one more glower down the length of my body and adjusts his cock in his pants before he stalks out and I hear the front door slam.

Titus

. . .

I OPEN the distributor and remove the rotor on Sunny's bus, just in case she's serious about leaving. I don't think she will, but the woman is pretty stubbornly independent.

And it wouldn't be the first time she's run off on me.

I rub my forehead as the testier part of me grumbles that I should let her leave if she wants to leave. I'm not looking to get tangled up with her again anyway. But there's no way I can let her fend for herself like this.

A few days until she's out of pain and I can get her bus repaired. Then we can part ways before things get intense again.

It's the only decent thing I can do.

I walk over to the diner and pick up three orders of the huevos rancheros (two for me, because I have a wolf's appetite), and I get a couple giant bear claw pastries too.

My wolf gets cheerful on the walk back, like the idea of providing for a female makes him frisky.

She's not our female. Definitely not our mate, I tell him, but he doesn't give a shit. In fact, he was ready to mark her this morning the moment I caught the scent of her arousal. Which doesn't make sense. I never even marked Barbara, Titus Junior's mother. Just never had the urge. She wasn't my true mate.

In retrospect, I don't even know why I took her as a mate. I think it was because she wanted it from me.

I got sucked into her world.

Or maybe because I wanted a kid.

I did want Titus Junior, even though it sucked raising

him without a mother or a pack. He's the only thing that ever made sense in my life.

Fates know females never did.

I open the door, and sniff the air.

She's still here.

I'm surprised at how relieved I am. This woman gets under my skin far too quickly.

I bring the food into the bedroom, and I'm instantly hit by her scent. She's still aroused. Moreso, even, than when I left.

What turned her on? Being tied up? Anticipation of a reward? I vow to get to the bottom of it, but after I feed her.

"Were you good while I was gone?"

"Nope," she says immediately. "I was definitely not." She squirms around on the bed.

Fuck. She's so hot like that.

I set her free and help her sit up, then place the food in her lap.

"Thank you," she purrs. "This smells amazing." Because she's Sunny, I know she means every bit of the glow of appreciation she infuses into her words.

My wolf preens.

I get us forks from the kitchen and perch on the side of the bed to eat with her. I don't know why—I could just as easily leave the food with her and eat mine at the table, but it's like I have to watch her eat the food I brought home.

For one moment, I imagine how it would've been to have Sunny as the mother of my pup instead of Barbara.

I somehow know she would've cried over the pup,

never would've wanted to let him out of her arms. Not like Barbara, who barely bonded with our son.

"Are you thinking about babies?" Sunny asks with that uncanny habit she has of reading minds.

I screw my face up into a grumpy mask. "What are you talking about, woman?"

"You want grandbabies, too, don't you? I seriously can't wait."

I throw her a dubious look. "Why? What's the rush?"

Her tongue darts out to lick a speck of salsa from her lips and my dick gets hard. "I love babies. I can't wait to be a grandma, although I'm not going to let them call me that, of course."

"*Them*?" I chuckle. "You have this all planned, don't you?"

She shrugs.

"Why did you only have one kid, if you love babies so much? Couldn't fit any more into that RV of yours?"

Like a light bulb on a dimmer switch, I see the light around her face diminish.

Damn. I'm such an asshole.

"I tried." The two words drop and sink between us like blocks of concrete into a lake. She shrugs, her gaze taking on a remote look, like she needs the distance to speak them. "Five miscarriages. Foxfire is the only baby I brought to term."

A chill runs across my skin.

"Shit." I can't imagine. I remember the anticipation of Tank's birth. If the pregnancy had ended in tragedy, I don't know how I would've gone on. "I'm sorry. That sucks."

"Yeah, well, I got Foxfire." Her voice is falsely cheerful. She's a terrible actress.

"Were they all… with the same guy? With Foxfire's dad?"

Half-breeds are weaker species, maybe that was why. Or maybe Foxfire was the only one who took *because* she is half shifter.

A shutter slams down over her features. "No. Didn't you have work to do today? Private business or something?"

Wow. Okay. Touchy subject.

And she's right. I have shit to do.

I shouldn't feel offended at being shut out by an overly-emotional woman I didn't want to get involved with, anyway.

I can't stop the sympathy swimming through me, though. Sunny comes off as chirpy cheerful, but that doesn't mean she hasn't suffered, just like the rest of us.

"I do need to head out. You're going to stay here and heal. Right?"

"Yeah, okay."

"Do not leave this place. If you need something, text me. Understand?"

"Yeah, yeah. Got it." She waves me away.

I don't like the way it feels. My wolf wants her to accept my protection. To receive what I'm offering.

But that's stupid.

I can't offer her anything.

I pick up the empty cartons from breakfast and stand. "Need anything before I go?" I'm disturbed that I have the urge to lean down and kiss her goodbye.

Not my mate. *Not. My. Mate.*

"No, thank you, Titus. I'll be fine."

I nod and leave, both relieved and disappointed to leave her.

❧

Titus

I HEAD INTO TOWN, not even sure how I'm going to go about finding Buzz. Taos is a small town, but I know instinctively that asking around will yield nothing. Buzz is the kind of guy who wouldn't want people asking or talking about him. Anyone who's friends with him would know that and; therefore, wouldn't give out information.

I'm better off just sniffing around. Letting my instincts guide me. I had a good feeling out at the gorge, maybe I should start there.

That was because of her, my wolf says.

Shut up.

Yeah, I'm talking to myself now.

I get on my bike and head out for the high bridge, but keep riding until I reach the Carson area. My skin prickles with warning.

I drive out to a convergence of towns, an area called Three Points, and there, at a corner, I see the goddamn vehicle that ran into Sunny last night.

"Hey!" I shout.

The guy looks at me through the windshield, and then he guns it, taking off at top speed.

Rage rushes through me hot and fierce.

This guy hurt Sunny. I am going to pound him into a pulp. I zip after him, the bike roaring beneath me. We hit seventy miles an hour. Eighty. Ninety.

If this asshole thinks he can outrun my Harley, he's out of his mind.

He skids around a turn and I gain on him, but he's approaching some kind of settlement.

There's not a better word. We're out in the middle of nowhere, but several acres of land are pocked with shacks, RVs, buses and other temporary housing units. Cars are parked everywhere in traveling circus meets *Deliverance*.

The car skids to a stop and mangy men emerge from everywhere. The hair stands up on the back of my neck as my instincts scream danger. Two dozen or more of them, all coming out to see what the commotion is.

I pull up and park the bike, getting off and going to them before they come to me.

I'm aware that I'm grossly outnumbered.

The scent of shifter hits me hard, and I realize now the extent of danger I'm in. With my strength and resiliency, I could've handled a big group of humans. Not true of shifters. They will know how to take me down.

I lift my nose to the air, trying to identify their species. They're too mangy for wolves.

As they advance, it hits me: coyotes.

Fucking coyotes.

"Can I help you?" the asshole driving the car that hit Sunny asks.

Ignoring the danger, I go alpha on him. I stalk around the car and plow my fist into his face. Bone crunches under my fist and his body flies back and dents his car door.

The rest of the pack surge forward, making a tight circle around me, but no one touches me.

Yet.

Pack laws must be similar. Direct challenges are generally honored among shifters. Settling things physically has always been our way. And if they haven't caught my scent yet, they'll know by the way I handled this asshole that I'm not human.

The guy must pick up that I have a personal beef because he swipes at the blood coming from his nose. "What's your problem?"

I point at the smashed in front of his car. "Hit and fucking run is my problem. You nearly killed a human I care about." I swing again and he ducks and swings back. His fist hits my ribs but doesn't make much of an impact.

I slam him into the car with a chokehold around his neck. Now that I look at him closer, the guy looks twitchy to me—small pupils. Sweaty. Like he's on drugs. Great, just what I need. A tweaked out coy dog.

Growls start up all around me when he turns purple and his eyes bulge.

I release him and land a couple more punches.

"That's enough." I recognize the alpha command and take a step back. I'm not crazy enough to know they couldn't easily take me down. A skinny, bearded man steps into my space. "Who are you?" he demands.

"I'm Titus. And I demand restitution."

I don't know if this is gonna get me anywhere. Some

packs follow strict codes of conduct, others are more loosely governed.

"Wolf." The coyote alpha spits. "Haven't seen you around before."

"Well, I'm here now. Demanding restitution."

The alpha considers me for a moment. Then turns to the driver of the car. "This true? You hit a human with your car?"

The guy shrugs. "I hit a *VW bus*."

"With a human female inside. She's injured and the vehicle needs repair. You're going to fucking pay for it." I jab a finger in his face and the pack growls around me.

I wait two breaths before I drop my finger. I'm not gonna show submission to a pack of coyotes, even if they could rip me apart.

"The human's alive?" the alpha asks after a beat.

"Yeah. Broken arm. Lacerations."

He considers me for a long moment. "She can bring the bus here. We'll repair it for her." He jerks a thumb in the direction of one of the falling down buildings. It looks like an old gas station.

Fuck. Is he telling me they're mechanics? I'm torn between not trusting Sunny's vehicle with these guys, and wanting justice.

"No chance in hell I'm sending her here. He can come pick it up. And deliver it in perfect condition. And pay the hospital bill."

"We'll fix the vehicle. Hospital is your problem."

I whirl and face the alpha fully, fingers curling into fists. Growls start up again. I'm ready to throw down over the hospital bill, but it occurs to me that you can't bleed a turnip. These guys don't look like they're swimming in dough.

Looks like another shit pie is getting served up.

It also occurs to me that I'm here to do a job for my pack. One I seem to have completely forgotten.

"Picked up and delivered," I insist.

"Fine." The alpha waves a hand at me.

I force my fists to unclench and try to relax the scowl from my face. "Permission to speak to you about some unrelated business."

The alpha's brows shoot up. "What is it?"

"You know anything about a lab out this way? Or shifter disappearances in these parts?"

The guy snorts. "You'd know more about that shit than I would." He turns on his heel and walks off.

What does that mean?

"Hold up," I call out, but the coyotes close ranks behind him, blocking my path.

Fuck.

I snarl directions to the hit-and-run asshole and get back on my bike. As I ride away, I breathe in the smell of hot sage to take the coyote stench out of my nose.

SUNNY

I'M UP, showered, and sitting on the couch reading on my Kindle app when Titus returns.

"I found the guy who hit you."

A car pulls into the drive and a scrawny guy with a t-shirt stained with blood tumbles out of the passenger side.

"Titus... what did you do to him?"

"I busted his nose," Titus answers like it was the only logical action he could've taken. "And I told him he'd better fucking fix your bus. So he's here to take it. Toss me the keys."

My mouth drops open. I'm not sure what I think. Whether Titus is a hero or someone I really should distance myself from. Violence isn't something I condone.

I do appreciate him arranging to have my VW fixed, though.

I pull out my keys and then hesitate. "What if he steals it?" I mean the guy looks totally sketchy. Definitely a tweaker. That's probably why he left the scene of the accident. He was under the influence and knew he'd get busted.

"Then I'll kill him," Titus says loud enough for the guy standing outside to hear.

A shiver runs down my spine, because I can't tell how serious he is. Still, I trust him to handle this. I toss the keys.

He catches them in his huge hand and heads outside.

Sexy, capable man. I'm long past experiencing the biological urge to find a worthy provider, but my hormones don't seem to know that. I swear my ovaries just dropped three fresh eggs.

When Titus returns, he catches sight of the flower arrangement I made with a jar out of the recycling bin out back and the flowers growing around the cottage.

"Who brought those?" he demands.

"I picked them outside."

"Huh." He looks at the jar for a long moment, then at me.

I'm expecting him to rant about me leaving the bed, but instead he cocks his head like he can't understand why I would do such a thing.

"You like flowers?"

I laugh. "Of course. Who doesn't? I love flowers."

"Huh," he says again, like he thinks it's the weirdest thing. "I guess that's what artists do, right?"

"What?"

"Bring beauty to our world."

I laugh, deflecting the compliment. "The beauty was already in our world, I just brought it inside."

"Yeah, I guess." He turns the jar around like it's the most curious thing he's ever seen.

Maybe it is weird—I don't know. It's just what I've always done. A surface without a jar of flowers always looks bare to me. "That's the major downside about living in an Airstream. I don't get to plant my own cutting garden." I climb off the sofa. I haven't taken the pain meds they gave me—I didn't even want to fill the prescription but Titus insisted. My head throbs, and I stop my forward motion for a moment.

"Why are you off that couch, little lady?"

I hide my wince at the spinning room and throw a hand out to catch myself against the door. "Don't call me lady."

"Right. Yeah." Titus frowns at me, glaring at the bump on my head. "I shoulda broken that guy's arm before I left," he mutters.

"Titus, no. I don't want violence enacted on my behalf. I appreciate your help, but please. No more."

The room tilts and I'm suddenly in his arms. "I think I told you to stay resting." The deep rumble of his voice enters my chest and heats me from the inside out.

"I don't like staying in one place for too long."

He carries me to the bedroom. His beard tickles my cheek.

"Besides, I'm hungry. Let's go get some lunch, Titus. I'll buy."

"You need to stay put." He lowers me gently to the bed. "I'll get lunch."

"Titus—"

"Hush or I'll tie you to that bed again."

"That would sound hotter if you weren't so cranky. Last time was a supreme disappointment, I'll have you know. I thought something fun was going to happen."

Titus' head snaps up, his gray eyes lock with mine.

Oops. I probably shouldn't reveal how turned on I was this morning. But seriously. The guy tied me to the bed with his belt. I don't know how kinky he is, but I sure as hell thought something more was going to happen than him setting me free when he returned with breakfast.

He growls, stalking back to the edge of the bed. "Now you're just begging for trouble."

Excitement zings through me at the gruff growl of his voice. My lady parts perk up. Is it wrong to want to have sex with him even when I know he's not into getting involved with me?

Maybe.

I could end up with a broken heart, here. But only if I

put my heart in play. And I don't have to. I can just look at this as a chance to indulge in a little pleasure. Something I haven't had enough of, frankly.

Especially from a man who gives it the way I like it—wild and rough.

Titus grabs my hips and drags me down on the bed. He rolls my hips to the side and slaps my ass. "A supreme disappointment, huh?"

I smile up at him, heart picking up speed. "Supreme."

He glowers at me but I notice his cock's at full mast, bulging in his worn jeans. "You're just hours out of the hospital, with a busted arm and a bruise the size of my fist on your head. Did you really think you were up for sex with me? I would break you in two, little girl."

I let out a chuff, because it's true. I'm still sore from the pounding he gave me before the accident. In many places. But I don't back down. "I'm not hurt below the waist." I reach between my legs and run my middle finger over the crotch of my yoga pants, stopping at my clit and rubbing.

He stiffens, eyes locked on my movements. "Babydoll, you're asking for way more trouble than you can handle."

"So you keep saying."

He lunges.

Rips down my yoga pants and pushes my two knees to one side. "You don't know when to let up, do you?" He slaps my ass four times, hard.

I yelp and squeal, attempting to wriggle, but he has me pinned. My body floods with endorphins—the pain of the spanks instantly morphing to pleasure. Heat building in my pelvis.

His breath is ragged, movements jerky. He slaps me twice more, then peels my knees open.

I moan an invitation.

He slides his hands under my buttocks and cups my smarting cheeks, squeezes and kneads them as he lowers his head between my legs.

For one tortuous moment, he just inhales, like he enjoys the scent of my musk. Then he licks into me.

I warble my approval—somewhere between a gasp and a cry. My pussy contracts, flames of desire burn brighter.

Titus' beard tickles my inner thighs, chafes my labia. His tongue is magnificent. Big and strong and hot like the rest of him. And he knows how to use it. He teases and tortures me, circling my inner lips, flicking my clit. He stiffens his tongue and penetrates me with it, all the while using his nose to grind over my clit.

I writhe beneath him, coils of lust twisting tighter and tighter. Need winding up.

"I want you in me," I tell him. I'm past the point of pretending I don't know what I want in bed. Besides, I don't have it in me to reciprocate with oral today and I want him satisfied, too.

He growls. His eyes are bright blue. He rises up on his knees, peels off his shirt and unbuckles that belt again. Damn, it's sexy.

I sit up to help, but he flattens me on the bed with a hot kiss. "You gotta tell me if it hurts," he breathes against my lips. "I'm not good at gentle."

I lift my hips to meet his cock, run it through the tunnel of inner thighs and wet pussy. His erection grows even longer. "I'll use the stoplights." I nip his lower lip.

When he backs away and frowns, I laugh. "Green means go. Yellow is caution. Red is stop. It's a BDSM thing."

"I don't know what the fuck you're talking about," he mutters, but I'm beyond caring because he's dragging the head of his cock through my juices.

"Green, green, green," I chatter, undulating my hips to rub back.

He barks a curse and spears me with a single thrust.

I cry out when my head hits the headboard.

"Fuck." He pulls out.

"No, no, no, no. Don't stop, Titus. Please. I need this. It will help me heal."

I would say anything right now to get him back inside me, but it probably will. I believe in orgasms as a method of improving all kinds of things, including world peace, sexual healing and saving the planet.

"You sure? I don't think this is a good idea."

I reach for his cock and pull him back between my legs.

"Fuck." He drags me down the bed and shoves in again, this time pinning a fist above my shoulder to keep me from sliding up. He shakes his head as he rocks into me. "You are the strangest female I've ever met."

I'm used to this.

Believe me, I'm used to it.

But it's not exactly what I want to hear during coitus. Call me old-fashioned.

He must see it on my face, because he changes to short, upward thrusts and lowers his head to my breast. "Sorry, sunshine. I didn't mean that like it sounded." He bites my nipples over my shirt, then shoves the fabric up and swirls his tongue over them.

I forgive him because—yeah—it feels great. I tilt my pelvis to take him deeper, squeeze my muscles around his cock.

"Fates, woman, you learned that trick in yoga, too?"

"Uh huh. I can lift my leg above my head. Want to see?"

"Fuck yes. But next time." His knuckles brush my cheek. "Don't want to jar your arm."

I grip his shoulder with my good hand to feel the steel of his muscles as he picks up speed.

"What color?" he rasps. His eyes are such a bright shade of blue. I see his spirit animal so clearly now, shimmering beneath the surface.

A beautiful silver wolf.

"Green. Still green. Don't stall, Titus."

He lets out a snarl. I almost don't see his human face anymore, just the wolf glimmering in my third eye. This is some kind of wild mating dance to the wolf. He's a predator. I'm the prey. The sex is the chase and he's so close to catching me…

"Sunny…" He pounds into me with brutal force, his face twisted with unspent desire.

I realize he's waiting for me. "I'm ready to come," I gasp. "Give it to me, Titus."

He roars and bucks even harder.

My eyes roll back. I hear the plaster of the wall busting under the force of the bed slamming against it.

Titus comes.

I follow, my body perfectly synchronized to his. My internal muscles squeeze and milk his cock.

The wolf bares its fangs.

I scream when his head descends to my neck, eyes gleaming, teeth unnaturally sharp.

"Titus!" I shove him away with both hands and pain shoots through my broken arm. "Red," I yelp. "Ow, fuck."

Titus rears back, all the way off the bed. His tongue touches his teeth and his eyes fly wide. "Shit."

I'm shaking all over. "Wh-what was that?"

"Nothing," he says quickly, turning his back as he gets dressed. "I'm sorry I got too rough."

Too rough.

That wasn't it.

It was more like the veils between dimensions blurred for a moment there. Something from the spirit world tried to cross over.

And bite me.

But that doesn't make sense.

That doesn't happen.

I just had a very realistic vision, that's all.

"I-I saw your spirit animal," I try to explain. "It was so real it scared me."

Titus stabs his fingers through his hair. "Oh yeah? What animal?"

"Wolf. I've told you that before. A silver wolf with…" I look sharply at his eyes, but they aren't the bright blue of the vision, they are slate gray, like usual.

"With what?" he looks wary.

"Nothing. Nevermind. Sorry. I'm just being… strange again."

Like he needed more evidence of my whack-o-ness.

~

Titus

FATES. I can't believe I just tried to mark Sunny.

A human.

That doesn't happen. That shouldn't happen. Something's seriously off with my wolf if he's picking a human to try to mate with. After all these years, after him never choosing to mark Barbara, the mate *I* chose.

It's insanity.

The worst of it is Sunny somehow knew. I don't know what she sensed, but she screamed right when I was about to sink my serum-coated teeth into her flesh to forever mark her with my scent.

A bite that could be fatal on a human.

Fuck.

And now she's scared.

And possibly hurt.

"You're not strange," I lie. My rational mind tells me not to get within ten feet of her, but the scent of confusion and pain fills the room, and there's no way I can heed my own warning system.

She touches the goose egg on her forehead. "You know, I think I'm just hungry." Her words come out shaky, but I don't call her on the lie.

I'm not up for unpacking the whole shifter thing with

her right now. Especially not the fact that I almost marked her.

Something is seriously off with my wolf.

"I'll get you some food."

"No." She swings her legs off the bed and pulls on her clothing. "I can't stand being cooped up so long. I'll go with you."

Of course. I knew she was flighty as hell. I can't even keep the woman resting for half a day.

I pinch the bridge of my nose. "Fine. A short outing. What are you in the mood for?" I seriously hope it's not some kind of vegan shit.

"I could go for a big, juicy burger."

Be still my heart. Maybe she isn't so weird after all.

"Me, too, sunshine. Let's go."

CHAPTER 4

 *unny*

TAOS IS one of those small towns where you always know
someone anywhere you go. The diner is no different.

I know Rebecca, our server, from yoga and authentic
movement classes. Her eyes widen when she sees me
come in with Titus. Well, nearly everyone has to look at
him when we come in. He is pretty attention-grabbing. The
huge, truck-like frame, the leather jacket. The silver beard
and rugged good looks. He's beautiful, and they know he
must be new in town because they would've remembered
seeing him before.

She bustles over to our table. Only then does she peel
her eyes off Titus and sees the bump on my head. "What
happened to you?"

"Hit and run." I grimace and hold up my casted arm.

She gasps. "Oh no! That's horrible." Her eyes dart to Titus again with a question in them.

"This is Titus, my son-in-law's father. Thank goddess he was here when it happened. He's taking good care of me."

Rebecca beams at him. "That's great. I'm glad he was here, too."

We order burgers. Titus orders mine with a gluten-free bun—I'm so touched he remembered—and fries. When they come, Titus squirts a huge pile of ketchup on my plate first, then his own.

They are simple, tiny gestures, but sweet. I'm not used to having anyone try to take care of me. Part of me hates it—I don't *want* to depend on anyone. I got hurt in my first marriage —badly—and I don't ever want to be in that position again.

But I can't deny the appeal.

"I wouldn't have pegged you for a burger and fries kind of girl," Titus says, stuffing several fries in his mouth at once.

"No?" I laugh. I guess when we hung out before, we didn't do much eating out. I seem to recall we just ordered in a lot of pizzas and Chinese food. "Yes, I like meat."

Titus growls at my smirk.

I stare at his plate, stunned to see he's already eaten his first burger. I take a bite of my french fry. "So I thought you worked a security job, back in Wolf Ridge."

"That's right. I work night shifts at the brewery there."

"So what assignment brings a security guard to Taos?"

He considers me, then shakes his head. "I can't discuss it."

I persist because it doesn't make much sense. "Brewery business?"

"I'm following up on some criminal activity."

"What kind?"

"What part of *I can't discuss it* did you not get?"

I hold up my hands. "Okay, okay. Touchy. Secret brewery business, then."

He rolls his eyes.

I wipe my lips with my napkin. "Do you think you could drive me out to my RV?"

He raises a brow. "Excuse me?"

"Because I don't have the bus. Could you give me a ride to my place?"

He blinks at me for a few beats. "I rented that goddamn place so you'd stay put and rest. Are you seriously telling me your wanderlust has already kicked in? You can't stay still for more than half a day?"

I sense so much judgment in his words, and I hate to admit how much it hurts. I look down at my food, suddenly not hungry.

"Seriously, what's the rush?"

I snap my head back up. "I don't get paid to lie around on your sofa, Titus. If I'm not making art or selling it, I don't eat. That's the reality of my situation."

He shakes his head. "And who picked that situation?"

I throw down my napkin and scoot my chair back. "I didn't ask for your help, Titus. I don't need it. I also didn't ask for your judgment of me or my lifestyle. Don't worry about giving me a ride, I can find my own way home." I dig in my purse for some cash and drop enough to cover both our meals on the table. I'm not about to let Titus do anything more for me.

"Now wait up." He rises, too. "I'll drive you. Just hold your horses."

I hold up my hand. "No, really, Titus. I'm good. Thanks for everything." I lean over to kiss his cheek to prove I'm not pissed—which I am. I just don't want to be. I don't want to care what this giant, manly monster of a man thinks of me.

I don't want to fit into his rigid mold of how things should be. Or how they shouldn't.

Yes, I'm unique. I've always been different. Even as a child, the other kids thought I was weird. I suppose that's why I married so young. I was just so eager to be with someone I thought wanted and accepted me.

But my first marriage couldn't have been more painful.

I walk out into the unfiltered sunshine of high-altitude living. Taos isn't the kind of place you can grab an Uber, but if I walk around the plaza, I'll eventually bump into someone I know who I can ask for a ride out to my RV.

Of course, then I'll be stuck out there with no way of getting back into town if I need something. Maybe I didn't think this through quite carefully enough when I made my request.

Maybe Titus was right.

Maybe I was running away again. From him.

From the vulnerability he evokes in me. Just look at how easy it was for him to hurt me and I wasn't even giving over my heart!

No, I made the right choice. Distance is definitely the best option.

In desperate need of a mood lifter, I slip into Adele's chocolate shop. The rich scent of cocoa rolls over me as the tall proprietress straightens from behind the counter.

"Hey, Sunny," she calls out, her wide mouth breaking into a smile until she gets a good look at my banged up face. "Oh my God, what happened?"

"Car accident. Hit and run. I could really use a pick me up." It's true, although it's not because of the car accident.

"Oh, I have the perfect thing for you, my friend. Taste this." She slides a plate with three truffles across the counter. "My latest creation. Apricot sea salt truffle."

I pop the little morsel in my mouth and groan. "Yes. This was exactly what I needed." I close my eyes and savor the explosion of flavor in my mouth. "Exquisite. You truly have a gift, Adele."

"Why does it look like your boyfriend is standing guard outside?"

"My boy—" I start to turn, but stop myself. "Oh. Titus is outside?"

Adele tucks an errant black curl behind her ear and gives me an assessing look. "Are you not into him? I kinda thought you guys had chemistry?"

"Oh we have chemistry all right. That's sort of the problem."

"How is that a problem?"

I lean my elbow on the counter and put my chin in it. "Makes it harder to keep my distance. Especially because the sex is so good."

"Ah. So the sex is great but the personality isn't there?"

I pop another truffle in my mouth. "I like his personality, too. I just… Well, I'm too much for him. Story of my like… I mean, life."

Sympathy flickers over Adele's expression before she hides it. "Never make yourself small for a man," she says firmly. "You keep on living loud and proud, being who you are. The guy who's man enough to let you be you will show up."

My eyes smart, but I blink it away. "Yep," I agree, because I'm only capable of speaking the one syllable without letting out a warble in my voice.

"As for this guy… if you need help shaking him—"

"Oh, no." I wave a hand. "He would back off if I made it clear that's what I wanted." But it's not what I want. That's the problem. "I'm sure he'll leave on his own soon enough." The words taste sour. I select another truffle.

"When things end, you'll still have your friends," Adele murmurs. "We'll all be ready to order a bottle of wine and commiserate."

"Thank you, dear. Time heals all lies… I mean, wounds." I stuff the third truffle into my mouth before I mix any more metaphors. "Ahem. What do I owe you?"

"Oh these are on the house."

I smile, somewhat relieved because her truffles are damn expensive. As they should be—they're the finest thing I've ever put in my mouth. "Thank you so much, darling. Well, I'd better get out there and see if I can't lose my bodyguard."

"Eh. Use him for the sex. You deserve it."

I laugh. "Already have!" I sing out as I leave.

Titus is leaning up against the doorframe with his arms

crossed over his massive chest and a first class scowl on his face.

I ignore him and sail past.

He gives a low growl, but doesn't touch me, just follows a step behind.

I wind my way through the plaza, stopping to greet and chit chat with friends, knowing I'm driving Titus bonkers.

It's his choice to make himself my babysitter. Eventually, I end up sitting down on a bench because I hit the end of the line, and I don't have a plan yet for getting to my RV.

Titus looms over me, blocking the harsh angle of the sun. He sticks his hands in his pockets, which is a decidedly non-dominant pose. Apparently, he's making an effort to appear conciliatory.

I look up.

"I'm going to drive you out to your RV now," he mutters.

I purse my lips. It's on the tip of my tongue to refuse, but that would be the definition of cutting off my tongue to spite my nose. Or whatever the saying is.

Instead, I stand. He hesitates like he wants to say something, but then just tilts his head toward the parking lot where we left the Harley and waits until I start walking to fall into step with me.

He's smart enough not to touch me or to say anything. In fact, neither of us say a word during the walk to the bike.

"I'm parked out on Cebolla Mesa," I tell him.

He shakes his head, unfamiliar with the area. I give

him directions and accept his helmet before I climb on the back of his motorcycle.

I wrap my arms around his washboard abs—the best I can with the cast—and try not to think about how easily my body sinks into pleasure just touching him. I try to ignore the thrill of the speed on the bike and the expert way he handles it.

No, this hedonistic pleasure that Titus incites can't be trusted. I was smart enough to walk away last time.

I need to do the same thing now.

Titus

I OUGHT to be glad Sunny's through with me. I called her on her shit and she walked, same as last time.

But there's something itchy and unsettled in my center. Like I fucked up and I need to fix it.

So my compromise is making sure Sunny gets safely to her RV instead of wandering around the plaza like a vagabond.

The drive to her RV is beautiful and the place she chose to park exquisite. She's nestled right on the edge of the Rio Grande gorge, but still among pine trees.

She has a couple solar panels on the roof, a solar shower set up in a tree and a little flower pot with wilted columbines by the front door.

"Oh, you're thirsty, aren't you, sweet flowers? Let me give you a drink." The looney woman is talking to her flowers. She opens the RV and comes back out with a jug of water, which she pours on the wilted flowers. "The pot is too small," she says to me, as if I was wondering. "It dries out too quickly and with me not coming home last night..." She pops back into the Airstream.

I want to go, but I feel uneasy about leaving her here. I know she's a grown woman and she's been living on her own forever, but it strikes me as extremely unsafe. She's a fragile human female, out here in the wilderness, where no one could hear her scream.

I circle around the RV, lifting my nose to scent the air. I wish I were in wolf form, so I could really get a sense for what's been around here. I step into a thicket of trees and catch a scent that sends a shock through me.

Shifter.

Male wolf.

Who has been out here? My buddy Buzz?

Or could this have something to do with the lab I'm looking for? Maybe an escaped test subject.

I look back toward the RV, thinking about stripping to shift, but Sunny comes back out. "Don't feel like you have to hang around, Titus." It would sound rude, except she's wearing one of her bright sunny expressions. She truly was aptly named.

Reluctantly, I walk back. "Yeah, okay. I'll find out when your bus will be fixed. You need a ride out to the bridge tomorrow to sell your wares?"

"My stuff is in the bus. I wasn't thinking when you let him take it."

Shit. Now I feel like the biggest dick. And I sure as

hell don't trust those tweaker coyotes not to steal her stuff. And I'm affecting her ability to make a living.

"I'll go by and hurry them up," I tell her, even though it's a long drive out there. "And I'll let you know as soon as it's done."

She blinks those cat eyes at me. "Thank you, Titus."

"You need anything else?"

She puts her good hand on her hip but she's too nice to remind me that she already made it clear she needed nothing from me.

"Right. Okay. I'll be in touch."

"Thanks again!" She gives a cheerful wave.

I can't stand feeling like she's getting rid of me, but I know she is.

Damn.

I swing a leg over my bike and start it up. When I come back, I'm going to shift and follow those scents somehow.

Sunny

"Darling, I'm fine. Truly. Titus took good care of me." I called Foxfire as soon as I got settled. My RV functions perfectly off the grid with solar generated electricity to charge my cell phone. I just have to haul in my own water if I want to shower more than once a week because Taos only gets twelve inches a year of precipitation.

This is the first chance I've had to actually speak with

Foxfire, although we've texted all day.

"I still don't understand why Titus was there. Are you two… a *couple* now or something?" She sounds slightly nauseated by the thought. But children never like to think of their parents as sexual beings. Even with the sex-positive upbringing I gave Foxfire, she's squeamish about this.

"No!" My voice sounds too high-pitched. "He's here on business. I ran into him at the gorge bridge. And then he came to yoga."

Foxfire makes a spluttering sound like she just choked on a sip of water. "What? *What?*" She laughs. "Titus went to *yoga?*"

I chuckle too. "I know, darling. Ridiculous. See, there was this other man at the bridge and he said he was going—"

"Okay, stop. I'm not sure I want to know any of this."

"Well, you did ask, darling. I'm just trying to explain."

She makes a little discontented sound. "Does it involve you having sex with my husband's dad? Because I definitely don't want to hear about that."

"Okay, then the topic is now closed."

"Oh, Sunny! I didn't need to know!" she wails. My daughter has always called me by my first name because I wanted to parent her in a way that gave her full autonomy. I believe children, like all of us, are infinite beings. They're just trapped in tiny bodies and underestimated by the adults around them. I tried to function from the assumption that Foxfire had her full awareness and could make choices for herself, and I was just there to help and guide, when necessary.

I laugh. "Don't worry. I sent him on his way. I'm back

at my RV now, and I'm going to be fine as soon as I get my bus back. But enough about me. What's the status of my grandchildren?"

"Ugh, *Sunny!* Please."

"I want grandchildren, Foxfire. I sent you a little bag with moonstone and rose quartz to promote fertility."

"OMG, Sunny no. We don't need them."

"Oh, are you already expecting?"

"Sunny!"

"If you're having trouble, it might be Tank's sperm count. You can get a test to make sure."

"Do not mention my partner's sperm count ever again."

"Foxfire, you know how much I love babies."

Foxfire sighs but her voice softens. "I do know, Sunny. We're just not there yet."

"Well, don't wait too long, darling. I had such a hard time, you know. I just don't want you to pass your prime and then have the problems I did."

"Sunny. Don't project your fears onto me."

"You're right, you're right," I say immediately. I definitely believe thoughts create reality, and I shouldn't ever surround my daughter with my anxieties. "Surrounding you with unconditional love and the knowledge that you're perfect just as you are." This was the mantra I used to send her off to school with.

I hear the smile in Foxfire's voice. "Thanks, Sunny. I love you, too."

"Goodnight, darling. Give that man of yours a hug from me."

"Will do. Bye, Sunny."

 *itus*

I DON'T KNOW what in the fuck I'm doing. If I believed she was capable of it, I would say Sunny is truly a witch and she cast a spell on me.

But that's obviously not her speed. She's not looking to tangle anyone into her web.

Not intentionally, anyway.

Yet, tangled I am. That's the only explanation I have for why I feel it's necessary to drive her bus out to her with supplies in the back to make her flower boxes.

It's stupid, really.

I should just be dropping the vehicle off and then slink off to shift and sniff around her place to see what I can find. I have a job to do for Alpha Green.

Instead I'm set on playing gardener to a woman who doesn't want my help.

Fuck-nuts crazy.

And yet when Sunny bursts out the door in all her sunny glory when I pull up, I forget all my grudging reluctance. Her hair is pulled up on the top of her head in a messy bun that makes her look taller and more slender. The smile that stretches across her face could light a major city.

And just seeing her relieves some gnawing sense of wrongness I've had ever since I left her there last night.

"It's already fixed?" She bounds toward me. "That's wonderful!"

"I leaned on them a little bit." As in, I rode out there and stood over the fuckers until it was done. I'm probably lucky the pack didn't turn on me, but I got the sense the alpha had ruled this was my due, so the coyote had to comply.

Sunny gives me a quick peck on the cheek. I don't mean to, but my arm instantly bands around her and pulls that lithe body up to mine. "Oh!" The surprised little breathy sound makes my dick hard.

Or maybe it's having her frankincense and roses scent up in my nostrils. Or the soft give of her braless breasts.

"Busy this morning?" I grit out before I throw her over my shoulder and find a sturdy surface to fuck her on. A picnic table nearby would do, if it didn't have blocks of red clay and a large stick shaped item sticking up. Something about the shape makes me frown. "What the hell is that?"

"Oh." A splash of pink spreads between her freckles. "A little something I was working on. I was feeling inspired."

I pretend to examine the upright root. "What is it?"

"It's, ah, something I'm working on." She tucks a tendril of hair behind her ear and gazes at me with wide eyes. Slowly, my brain interprets the crude shape. I do a double take. Yep, the clay is shaped like a dick.

"The fuck?"

"Phallic art was very common in ancient civilizations. These models were symbols of fertility and thought to bring good luck." She raises her chin as she lectures me. "Anyway, I modeled it after you."

"Too small," I growl. I don't know what the hell else to say. Was she going to fire that clay and use it on herself? My cock's about to split my jeans. I turn away before I do something stupid, like sweep her art supplies to the ground and show her no clay model can compare to the real thing.

"Do you want it?" Sunny tentatively asks my back.

Hell no. I already got one, baby. "Keep it. Something to remember me by."

There's a long awkward pause while I think of sweaty football players to get my dick to calm down.

Sunny clears her throat. "So, do you need me to give you a ride back to town?"

Ouch. She's in a hurry to get rid of me.

Damn.

"Yeah. After I put something together." I open the side door of the bus and pull out the planters, potting soil and flowers.

Sunny gasps. "Titus!"

I don't look at her, because if I do, I'm afraid she's gonna end up on her knees in the dirt. With me banging her from behind. Instead, I grunt and stomp past, thunking down the heavy planters, one on either side of her door. I fill them half full with soil and then place the three different varieties of flowers the hardware store gardener recommended and tuck them into the planter. I repeat with the other side. The whole time Sunny's flitting behind me, making approving sounds.

I finish by packing the flowers in with more soil and stand up, brushing the dirt off my knees. "You have any water?"

I turn around and find Sunny already prepared with a plastic pitcher in her hand.

"Oh!" There's a slosh when our hands collide and water splashes over the front of her tank top. Her nipples poke through the thin fabric, hard and perky.

I try to look up. I really do. But the message isn't getting from my brain to my eyes. They are glued to those tight buds. My mouth waters. I clear my throat.

Neither of us moves. I'm not sure either of us breathes.

Three... two... one: My control snaps.

The pitcher crashes to the ground, splattering water over our legs. The RV nearly tips over with the impact of our bodies hitting the side. I claim her mouth violently at the same time I pinch one nipple between my thumb and forefinger.

She squeals her protest and I release my fingers, kneading her soft breast as I bite and lick down her neck.

"Come here," I growl, picking her up and carrying her inside.

Every pleasure center fires just having her in my arms, knowing I'm so close to claiming her.

I carry her to the mattress and lay her down, shoving

the tank top up to give her nipples more attention. I scrape my teeth over them, pinch and pull. Suck and kiss.

"Oh, Titus. You're driving me crazy."

The crazy is mutual, sunshine. And there's no other name for it, that's for sure.

"You want me to touch you here, baby?" I cup her mons, rub over her thin linen shorts. I'm trying to dial my aggression back and make sure she actually wants this. Especially considering she was busy getting rid of me when I arrived.

She wriggles against my hand. "No."

I go still.

Fuck.

"I want Spartacus."

"What?"

She pushes me back, straddles my legs and unzips my jeans. Releasing my cock, she grips me at the base. "This is Spartacus."

"Huh?"

"Your dick. I nicknamed it Spartacus."

"What? No."

"Spartacus." She gives me a stroke that makes my balls sit up and beg. "Because it rises to the occasion."

"What?" I fight to keep my train of thought. "Don't call it that."

"I'm Spartacus," she mock growls and then giggles.

"Stop. No."

But then she lowers her mouth and licks around the head.

"Yes. Hell yes, more of that."

"You like this?" She uses a mock innocent voice. Her cock-tease is making me lose my mind.

"Less talking, more sucking, woman," I growl.

"Okay, wolf." She takes me all the way into her mouth and the shudder of pleasure that rips through me nearly knocks over the RV.

Crazy fucking female, naming my cock.

As she sucks, I reach to unbutton her thin linen shorts and pull them off. It fucking kills me that she never wears panties. Makes her even more of a temptation knowing that pussy is *right there.*

I cup her pussy. When I rub my thumb over her slit, I find it sopping wet. Ready. "You want to get fucked by Spartacus?"

Fates, what's wrong with me? Now I'm calling my dick by her pet name, too. *Out loud.*

Ridiculous.

And kinda hot.

"Yes," she warbles.

I rise and switch places with her so I can drag my tongue from her entrance to her clit and back down again. She tastes like magic.

Moonlight and fairy dust. Flower petals and gemstones.

And that makes no fucking sense, so clearly I'm out of my mind.

I'm gonna blame the upcoming full moon for all this crazy. The full moon and this wild, wonderful woman beneath me.

I yank my jeans off. "You want him now?"

"Now." She claws my shirtsleeves and yanks me down over her, her lips parted.

Oh fates.

The world spins when we kiss. The earth shakes.

Oh wait, that might be the RV.

Or if it's not, it's definitely going to be soon.

I spear her with my erection, watching her expressive face contort with passion. Her eyes roll back in her head, mouth drops open. The moan she makes should be on autoplay for every porn video ever made.

"That's it, love," I croon, even though I've never been the sweet bedroom talk kinda guy. It just rolls off my tongue with ease.

I pull my hips back and shove in again, this time allowing myself to sink into my own pleasure. She feels so good. So right. She's small and human and I could split her in two with my massive erection, yet she receives every thrust with softness, with generosity.

She's the kind of woman who could give and give and give.

And I have no idea what makes me draw that conclusion, but I know it to be true.

"You feel so good, sunshine. So good."

"Conquer, Spartacus."

A laugh explodes from my chest. I brace myself on my fists beside her head and plow deep with hard rhythmic thrusts that definitely rock the Airstream.

She makes these crazy keening sounds. Desperate and needy and somehow appreciative.

I fuck her until she loses her mind and babbles

nonsense. I fuck her until I lose my mind. And then I pinch both her nipples at once and demand, "Come."

She does. Her pussy clamps down on my dick and then spasms as she climaxes.

I wait until she's done and push her to her side and shove her thigh up for a different angle. Perfection.

I ride her this way until I come, fireworks going off behind my eyes, the room somersaulting around and around.

When my vision clears, I fall down and wrap an arm around her waist. Spoon her. "I didn't know how badly I needed this," I confess.

Fates, what's wrong with me? I never talk about feelings and now I'm spilling everything? It's like I've been given truth serum or something. "I didn't know how good it would feel," I go on.

"Sexual healing, baby," Sunny says with a satisfied air.

I stiffen, images of her doing this with countless others running through my head. She's a free-loving, free-spirited soul born a little too late to join the hippie movement of the sixties.

"Easy, big guy." She rolls over. "Don't get jealous."

I don't know how she reads my mind like that. Witchy woman.

"How many?" I choke.

She places her good hand flat on my chest and swings a leg over my lap, straddling me. "Listen to me, Titus. You don't get to ask that."

"You're right," I say quickly. I'm way out of line. I don't know why I feel so damn possessive of this woman.

This woman who won't be claimed.

∿

SUNNY

TITUS THINKS I chose this lifestyle out of frivolity.

But the truth is, he's not the only one who left a relationship with a wound that never closed.

And even though I never talk about it, it feels important to tell him.

"All I ever wanted was to settle down and have a family."

Titus snorts, but when he sees I'm serious, he stills.

"I got married young. Just a year out of high school. To a nice young man. He was an actuary for an insurance firm. He wanted children—at least three. And he wanted to be the big man and support me to stay at home and raise the kids."

Titus stares at me with disbelief, like I might be making a long joke.

"I wanted kids for as long as I can remember. Since I was carrying around dolls at age three, probably, so it seemed perfect."

Titus gets tense. "What happened?" There's a warning growl in his voice, like he's going to go back and rip Jack's head off or something.

"We got married in a church with our family and friends and bought a little two bedroom house in Kansas City. I cooked and cleaned and planted flowers and waited to get pregnant."

I see comprehension dawn on Titus' face. Comprehension mingled with horror. He strokes a large, rough palm up my thigh. It's not sexual—more like he's trying to soothe me.

"It took a year and a half just to get pregnant. And believe me, we were trying. I took my temperature every morning, tracked my cycle. I knew when I was ovulating. I don't know what was wrong. The doctors couldn't figure it out. Eventually I got pregnant."

"And you lost it." The sympathy in Titus' gaze is almost too much to bear.

I blink rapidly. "Biggest disappointment of my life," I choke.

He squeezes both my thighs, then tugs me down to cover his body where he wraps me up in his arms. "I'm sorry, angel. It must've been awful."

"Yeah. My own private nightmare. After three more miscarriages, Jack couldn't take it anymore. He asked for a divorce and kicked me out. He remarried six months later and his new wife got pregnant immediately."

"Christ, Sunny." Titus' voice cracks a little.

I shrug against his chest. The sadness I buried so deeply, the one I've been running from all these years surfaces, but lying on Titus' strong chest makes it seem less consuming than it used to feel. "I had no college education. I didn't want to go crawling back to my parents, especially because they hadn't supported me marrying so young. I didn't want to hear *I told you so.*

"A friend of a friend who made jewelry for a living invited me to join her on the arts and crafts circuit. I helped her while I figured out what I could make that would sell and not compete with her, and I've been doing the circuit ever since."

"And then you met Foxfire's dad? What happened with him?"

"Johnny. Yeah. He wasn't the settle down and marry type. He was a very kind man. We had a spark immediately. Like you and me."

Titus' brow wrinkles but his gray eyes remain intent on my face and he doesn't interject anything.

"He had a really backwards family. Some kind of cult, really. And they wouldn't allow him to leave the flock or marry or anything. He was out selling wares on the circuit, too. That's how we met. We hooked up. It was his first time with a woman, and he didn't even think about condoms. I didn't insist because—well, I knew I'm not exactly Fertile Myrtle and he was obviously clean."

"But you got pregnant."

"Yes. We'd already parted ways when I found out, and he felt terrible. He talked about leaving his cult to come and live with me, but I didn't want that kind of pressure. I'd already had the picket fence and the provider husband and it sucked. The pressure to be perfect was too much to live up to, you know?"

Titus' jaw flexes. "Yeah, but he had a responsibility for the kit. I mean your little girl."

I laugh. "Did you call her a kit because of her name? That's so cute."

Titus' steel-gray gaze bores a hole through me.

"He did the best he could. He sent cash when he could scrape it together, but he was as poor as I was. I sent pictures. It worked out fine. Honestly, it's probably easier to raise a child on your own. No one to argue with about how they should be raised."

Titus shrugs. "True. Although I still don't get how a parent could live without their child. It's unnatural."

I tilt my head, noticing the clouds in his aura. "You never forgave her for leaving, did you?"

Titus stiffens, his abs going rock hard like he requires protection. I run my fingernails lightly down his chest, over his belly.

"No, I didn't. But she didn't just leave us. She cost me my job. My livelihood. She embezzled thousands of dollars from the company I worked for and then took off."

I can't hide my shock. "Wow. Total betrayal."

"Right."

"I'll bet you felt like you didn't even know who she was after she left."

He leans up on his elbows. "Exactly. How do you know that?"

I shrug. "I felt the energy of it. I'm so sorry, Titus. So you have to know it had nothing to do with you, right? That's just the kind of person she is. She would've done that with anyone."

"I was the idiot who decided to mate—I mean, marry her."

"No. Don't make yourself wrong. Your choice resulted in Tank. How can you possibly regret that?"

Titus' face softens. "You're right. Yeah. Totally." He scrubs a hand through his beard. After a beat, he says, "I get it now."

"What?"

"Why you won't settle down."

I hold my breath, not sure I want to hear his assessment of me. This is usually when I get my feelings hurt.

"You felt like you failed at it."

Tears spear my eyes. Titus lifts a hand and cups my cheek. "But the truth is, sunshine, you were perfect. I know you believe the Universe has your back and all that shit. Maybe the Universe just didn't want you to get stuck with that asshole raising pasty-faced weakling children. The Universe wanted you to have a big, bold bright daughter who is strong and as eccentric as you are."

I eyeball him. "I'm not sure if that was a compliment."

"Hell, yeah, it's a compliment. You did a fine job raising a child with smarts, grit, and the spirit of a warrior. So how can that be wrong?"

I grin at him like an idiot. He grins back. Then my stomach growls.

"Let's ride back into town and grab some lunch before you go out to the gorge," Titus offers.

"Yeah, okay." I climb off him, allowing the warm glow from his words to surround me. I pull on a little sundress and slip into a pair of sandals. For the first time with Titus, I feel like we might be on the same page, and I really like the way it feels.

Titus

AFTER LUNCH, Sunny leaves me at my place and heads out to the bridge to work.

I'm still anxious to get back and sniff around Sunny's RV in wolf form, but I'm going to wait until tonight. The moon is full. If there are other shifters around, they might be out on the hunt. I may find what I'm looking for.

In the meantime, I head into town and stop into the local dive bars, asking about my buddy Buzz.

No one's heard of him. And I don't get the sense they're lying, either. Maybe my friend isn't in these parts anymore.

I end up walking through the plaza. Everything reminds me of Sunny. The cantina where we had drinks. The place I was standing when I heard her car wreck. The roof where she gave me the worst cock tease of my life.

Where these thoughts used to grate on me, now all I feel is warmth for the beautiful human. Hearing about her past pain made it all clear to me now. She's been running to avoid the kind of rejection she received from her husband.

I want to smash his head in, even though I'm so glad she isn't married to him anymore. Still, the pain he put her through. She must've felt so inadequate and alone when he threw her out.

A growl comes from my throat and the tourists walking by skitter past.

I want to show Sunny she doesn't have to be afraid of rejection. She can settle down again. Not to raise a family, obviously, but to live in a real house. With flowerbeds.

And me.

Wait, no. That's crazy. I'm a wolf.

She's a human.

Relationships with humans are forbidden.

Look at Garrett, my wolf whispers. My alpha's son Garrett took a human mate. The excuse was that she's psychic. Has special abilities.

But my Sunny's special, too. She may not be full-on psychic, but she's certainly highly intuitive. She saw my wolf in her mind's eye. On some level, she knows what I am, she just doesn't have a context for it in this reality.

I find myself outside the chocolate shop where Sunny went the other day after we quarrelled, and I push through the door. A cheerful bell tied around the doorknob rings and Sunny's friend from yoga looks up with a smile.

"Oh, hi," she chirps. "You're Sunny's friend."

Is it weird that I'm pissed she didn't say I'm Sunny's man?

Definitely.

"Yes. I'm Titus."

"Adele." She sticks her hand out across the counter and I shake it. The place smells like sugar and chocolate and... the faint scent of coyote.

Please tell me she's not dating one of those low-life coyotes. Adele seemed way better than that. And that's saying something, since she's human.

"What can I get you?"

I do a quick sweep of the glass cases. "What, ah... what does Sunny like from here?"

A wide grin splits Adele's face. "Are you buying her a gift? I have just the thing!" She picks up a little box and uses the tongs to fill it with four perfect little truffles. They're like tiny art masterpieces. Too pretty to eat, really. "She will love this." She pops a lid on the box and wraps it up with a pretty ribbon.

I pull out my wallet. "How much?"

"Ten dollars, please."

Christ, ten bucks for four truffles. I guess they taste as good as they look. But I don't care. I would've paid fifty bucks for something that makes Sunny feel special. I hand over a ten dollar bill and accept the little box. "Thanks. I appreciate it."

I take the gift and walk out with a spring in my step. I made plans to see Sunny again tomorrow.

Tonight, I'll go out by her RV in wolf form and sniff around, but she doesn't need to know that. I'm hoping I get more information—anything of value—before I call my alpha with a report.

CHAPTER 6

 *unny*

THE LONG MOURNFUL howl of a wolf wakes me in the night.

The moon is full.

I hear coyotes all the time, but I've never heard a wolf before. I'm not sure how I even know it's a wolf, but I do. Living in an RV, it often sounds like animals are close— just outside the thin walls. I usually love it, but tonight a shiver runs up my spine.

Even though it's warm out, I pull the covers up to my chin.

I hear a stick crack beneath my window. The sound of panting.

Oh goddess, the wolf is right outside. A real wolf, not a spirit animal.

I sit up and pull the curtain aside to peer out. The

moonlight clearly illuminates a giant black wolf with glowing amber eyes. He's sniffing the ground around my RV.

My heart skips a beat.

Another wolf howls, farther away. The black wolf lifts its head and cocks its ears to listen. It stands still, waiting. Listening.

I hold my breath.

Another howl, this time closer.

The wolf bares its teeth and growls.

A silver wolf leaps from the thicket nearby and suddenly the two wolves are tangled in a snarling tumble.

I scream.

Nearby, the sound of growl-barks join the fray, like other wolves are closing in.

Another black wolf leaps from the woods and joins the tussle. Then two more.

I scream again; this time I get up and run outside. I don't know what I think I'm going to do—scare them off, maybe. Stop the fight.

One of the black wolves turns its white fangs on me with a snarl.

The silver wolf leaps from the fight with a snarl, landing between me and the black wolf, his back to me. His hackles stand up, his fangs flash in the moonlight. The sound coming from his throat is terrifying.

And yet it appears he's protecting me. Which makes no sense.

The four other wolves form a semi-circle facing us, growling, but then the biggest one sits, dropping its aggressive behavior.

It's clearly the alpha, because the other three immediately imitate the largest wolf, sitting.

The silver wolf continues growling and showing teeth.

It backs up, getting closer to me so I have to back up, too. The other wolves watch.

I don't know wolf behavior enough to understand what's happening, but I'm definitely scared.

The silver wolf backs up more, until its hind legs hit mine. Then it turns slightly and body checks me. Like it's trying to shoo me into the RV.

And that's when an unexpected name bursts from my lips.

"Titus!"

I stare at the wolf. I don't know what made me say it, but the energy is the same. This growling, fanged canine has the same gruff, protective quality Titus had when he dropped me off today.

But that makes no sense.

The big black wolf gets up and trots off like nothing just happened. It doesn't even bother looking back, as if it knows there's no chance the silver wolf will attack. The other three follow a moment later and I let out a shaky breath.

"Titus?" I whisper.

Am I going crazy? It's one thing to see a spirit animal —something from beyond the veil. It's another to believe an actual, real wolf is the same being as the man I was with earlier.

The wolf turns bright blue eyes on me.

My stomach flips.

It's the same wolf from my vision.

Definitely.

"Titus?" I try again.

And suddenly there's a blur of motion, a cracking of bones and the man stands before me.

Buck naked, cock erect.

Beautiful.

Raw power radiates from him.

Or is it magic? Because he's certainly something of the magical realm if he can change form at will.

I stumble back, suddenly frightened. I throw out a hand to catch myself on the RV. "Wh-what are you?"

His eyes still shine bright blue, not the slate gray they should be. His teeth still gleam extra white, canines too long.

"Get inside." His voice is raspy and rough, like he's forgotten how to talk.

I'm trembling, although I can't tell if it's from fear or something else. Anticipation. Desire.

Probably all of those things.

"Y-you're a wolf."

"Yeah." He advances on me, a predatory gleam in those blue eyes, and I'm forced to back up into the Airstream.

"Titus?"

It hits me suddenly.

Werewolves are real. He's a werewolf and the moon is full, which means...

Oh goddess, what does it mean?

"What happens to you when the moon is full?" My voice sounds as raw and scratchy as his now.

He catches the hem of the thin cotton nightshirt I was sleeping in and tugs it over my head. "Let's find out."

I'm naked. He's naked. The air charges between us, ready for the incendiary spark.

Most of my fear evaporates. If he's going to eat me, I don't think it will be in the Big Bad Wolf kind of way.

"Titus…"

His torso bumps into my chest as he crowds me against a wall. I don't know what I want from him—an explanation, a discussion. But he's not having it. He's still half-beast, and his wild side wants to get frisky.

Okay, then. I'm down.

All it takes is one touch.

When I grip his arm with my good hand for stability, he pounces, mouth descending for a searing kiss, arms scooping under my ass to pick me up. He carries me to the bed and falls onto it with me beneath him. His breath is hot against my neck as he drags his open mouth from my ear to shoulder. His cock wedges between my legs, skimming along the wet petals of my sex.

One thrust and he's in me—without either of us guiding the way. He pumps in and out, still kissing and sucking along my neck, my ear, my mouth. His tongue delves between my lips.

"Titus!" It seems to be the only thing I'm capable of gasping. I wrap my arms around his neck and rock my pelvis in concert with his, taking him deeper, receiving all the dangerous passion he brings.

Titus is always a rough lover. This time is no different, but there is a change. That underlying anger and frustration he usually brings is gone. He's stripped bare now, it's just his unchecked animal passion.

And he devours me.

Flesh slaps flesh, the RV rocks and creaks so loud I fear it will fall apart at the bolts. Everywhere he touches me brings searing awareness. He rises up to his knees and holds my hips, lifts and tilts me to the best angle and fucks hard.

I lose my breath. Even though my own need is off the charts, my body's pliant and yielding, instinctively reacting to his extreme aggression. It must know asserting my own will, trying to direct the action could result in pain. I submit, surrender to the sensations, the pleasure, the rushing in my body to meet him. Receive him.

He snarls. I see the wolf again, just below the surface. Not the real wolf, but his wolf spirit. This time I don't see it coming, His teeth sink into my shoulder the instant he comes.

It hurts but I hardly register the pain. It's the opposite of an out-of-body experience. I'm so in my body I'm awash with sensation. There's a rightness to the experience —like his teeth belong in my shoulder at the moment of orgasm. Like it's some ritual I've secretly known my entire existence but it only bloomed into my consciousness right now.

I climax, my eyes rolling back, pussy clenching and releasing around his cock.

And then I drift off—surfing the edge of consciousness and awareness of so many dimensions.

~

Titus

THE SHARP TANG of blood on my tongue brings me fully back.

Oh fuck.

What have I done?

"Baby?" I murmur softly, lapping at Sunny's wound with my tongue to speed the healing.

Thank fuck—I don't think I hit an artery. The blood loss is minimal and the wound doesn't appear too deep.

But I just violated pack law. First, I let a human see me shift, then I marked her. Both acts are forbidden. And the oldest of laws would require me to kill any human who knows about our kind.

Which obviously isn't going to happen.

But damn. I really screwed up. My alpha is going to have my head. I could lose my place in the pack—again.

Again, over a female.

But my self-flagellation has no place here right now. I need to take care of my female. She's injured and probably scared and confused.

"Was that a love bite?" she mumbles.

"What?" A choked laugh tumbles from my lips. My crazy, brilliant female. She doesn't even know what she knows.

"A love bite? Or am I going to turn into a werewolf now?"

I muffle a laugh, dropping my face into the crook of her neck and kissing along her hairline. "It doesn't work that way. We're a separate species. Not diseased."

"I feel so stupid," Sunny groans. "I kept seeing wolves and the whole time I thought they were spirit animals. Like the guys in motorcycle clubs share a similar spirit animal and that's what drives them together."

"Not stupid." I kiss her some more. "Incredibly intuitive. You saw what we try to hide."

She gasps and pushes me back so she can look at me. "Foxfire?"

I nod. "Half fox. It didn't manifest until she met Tank."

She covers her mouth with her hand. "Oh goddess! How could I not know this about my own child?"

"Not know?" Disbelief tinges my words. "You named her *Foxfire*. You definitely knew on some level. It just didn't fit into this reality so you didn't know how to categorize it."

Her eyes brighten with a sheen of tears and I stroke my thumb over her cheek, kiss her forehead. "I'm sorry I didn't tell you, sunshine. It's forbidden."

She nods and gulps. "I see. Yes. I understand." She blinks and I can practically see her mind whirring over everything that passed tonight. "And those other wolves tonight?"

My shoulders tense. "Shifters. I caught their scent earlier so I came back to sniff around in wolf form. There was a whole pack of them running around. My wolf went wild with the need to protect you."

Her eyes soften and the corners of her mouth lift for a moment before they drop again. "Do you think they meant me harm?"

I roll to my side, pulling her soft body against mine. Spartacus springs to attention like he's preparing for the

Olympics. *Down, boy.* "No. I thought they did, but as soon as they saw I was protecting you, they backed off. And they definitely could've taken me. It was four to one and they had youth and alpha command on their side."

"You don't know them?"

I shake my head. "There hasn't been a pack in these parts of New Mexico in twenty years. I know of one lone wolf in the area and I've been trying to scout him out. For whatever reason, the pack we just met is not public."

"So, what—there's like a public registry of packs or something?"

I can't stop the chuckle that bubbles up. It seems to be a recurring event since I marked Sunny. Like my wolf can calm down and enjoy himself now.

Dumb fuck doesn't even know we're long past mating age and he just marked a human, not a wolf.

"No, but the community is small. Packs convene with others in their region and hold annual runs to promote breeding. If we didn't, our species wouldn't survive. There simply aren't enough of us. So finding out there's some off-the-radar pack up here is suspicious."

Sunny touches the place I marked her and winces.

"I'm sorry for that. It won't happen again, I promise."

"Was it the full moon?" She blinks those wide, starry eyes at me.

I force a smile. "Yeah. A full moon thing." It's only a half lie. The full moon definitely contributed to me losing control of my wolf. I just don't need to tell her what the bite meant.

But that's stupid. If she mentions it to Foxfire, her daughter will be sure to explain. The mating bite embedded my scent into her skin. Permanently. She's marked as mine, and once a female is marked, her mate will follow her to the ends of Earth to be near her. To protect and provide for her. Whether she wants him to or not.

And in Sunny's case, I already know that's a *not*.

Plus, she's not a wolf, and I didn't have permission from my alpha to mate a human. The best thing I can do is pretend it didn't happen. Sunny would never want to be bound—she's far too independent for that. And mating her is a violation of pack code.

So if Sunny finds out what it means, she and I can discuss it then. But I'm not going to bring it up sooner.

"Titus?"

"Yeah?" I brush her hair back from her face. Her skin glows pale in the moonlight shining through the window.

She's like some kind of moon goddess. Lovely, delicate, ethereal. Not really of this world.

"Will you show me the wolf again? Please?"

I smile at the excitement in her voice. It's impossible to deny her this.

Still, I have to explain the laws. "You're not supposed to know, sunshine. It's forbidden to shift in front of humans."

"Please? Just one more time? He's so beautiful. I want to see the magic in motion."

I climb off the bed, shaking my head. "It's not magic. Just a different biology." I crack my neck and shift, dropping to all fours.

Her gasp does something to my pleasure centers. My wolf preens.

She sits up, her nudity glorious. My scent all over her, glorious. "Titus," she breathes. I put my paws up on the bed and lay my chin on her thigh.

"Oh goddess, you're beautiful." She strokes my ears, rubs my scruff. "Incredible."

I shift back and flop on the bed beside her. "Now you've seen. You must swear to never speak of it with another human."

"I swear," she breathes.

"Do you think you can refrain from letting on with the pack that you know? Even with Foxfire?"

"Oh!" She doesn't like that. I'm sure she wants to call Foxfire up right away to discuss it. "Well, of course I don't want you to get into trouble. I'll wait until she reveals it to me herself, then. I won't ever tell that I saw you shift. Pinky promise." She wiggles her pinky.

I chuckle and nip her finger instead of linking mine with it. "How's that broken arm of yours? I didn't hurt you during sex, did I?"

"Nope." She loops the casted arm around my neck and pulls me down onto her. My mouth mates with hers and I sink once more into pleasure.

Rafe

INTERESTING.

A lone wolf running in our territory.

Facing off with four of us to defend a human female. I

lead the pack back to our camp at the base of Taos Mountain.

A herd of deer lying between the school bus and the tent camp scramble up and bolt away, their fawns following on spindly legs.

Crazy fucking deer. They shouldn't be hanging around a wolf den. But Allison, the Snow White of misfit shifters, attracts every form of wildlife imaginable to our camp.

We shift in the mudroom, pulling on jeans and t-shirts before we step into a large but rustic cabin. At one time this was someone's winter retreat. Nestled just beyond Arroyo Seco on the way up to the ski valley, it's prime real estate. But we found it even more perfect to set up our operations here, and with our mercenary income, we could afford it.

"Who the hell was that?" my brother Lance voices the obvious question.

"Fuck if I know. Tourist, maybe," I venture.

"What's he doing with a *human*?" Deke spits. He's half feral. Killing comes a little too easily for him. I'm always watching him in case he loses his shit and becomes dangerous.

"I don't know, but I want you and Lance to keep an eye on him. I want to know why he's here and when he's leaving. Who the female is. Anything you can find out."

"Want me to rough him up?" Deke offers hopefully.

I shake my head. "Nah. Stay in the shadows for now. We don't want word getting out that we have a presence here. Especially with our current menagerie."

"Roger that, boss."

 *unny*

I WAKE up to the sound of clanging metal outside the Airstream. The soreness between my legs and the wound on my shoulder brings it all back.

Titus.

My wolf.

I slip on a short, thin robe covered with roses and step outside. The air still has the bite of morning chill and the smell of pine and sage fills my nostrils.

Titus has my bus jacked up and the tires off.

"Good morning." My voice is still rusty, which gives it a husky quality.

He looks over, his expression softer than I've ever seen it. "Morning to you, sunshine."

"What are you doing?"

"Rotating your tires. One of them needs a little air. I can fill it for you next time we're in town."

"I know how to—" I start to say, but he silences me with a frown.

I smile. Okay, he wants to help. Let him help. It's nice to have someone else to shoulder the burden for a change. I just don't want to get too used to it. Because Titus has already become someone I care about very much.

Someone it would hurt to leave.

Don't leave, then.

That's the whisper I hear in my head.

Last time I knew Titus wasn't ready for a relationship. And when we first bumped into each other at the bridge I still didn't think he was. But now?

After last night, now that he sees I've accepted him for who he is? Maybe things really could work between us.

Except... wait. It's forbidden for him to reveal himself to me. That probably means it's forbidden to be in a relationship, too. I open my mouth to ask, but stop myself.

I'm too happy this morning, still warm and glowy from having him in my bed. I don't want to ruin the moment and call an end to this thing we have going.

I'm sure it will come to its own natural conclusion. I don't need to rush things.

Except I don't want to lose my heart in the process.

Already lost, the whisper tells me. Well, better to have loved and lost than never have fucked at all. Never loved at all. Whatever.

I bang my hip on the doorframe as I head back into the Airstream to make Titus breakfast. Gluten-free banana walnut pancakes with fresh berries and cream. Unfortunately I don't have any meat in the fridge, but if I make enough pancakes it might satisfy him.

I chuckle out loud thinking about his appetite. No wonder he eats so much—a wolf's metabolism must be off the charts.

Forty minutes later, I set the picnic table with a pretty cloth and a jar of fresh wildflowers, then serve up breakfast. Titus shovels the food into his mouth enthusiastically. "This is good," he says between bites. "Real good."

"So are you really here on *wolf* business?" I ask.

He wipes his mouth with a napkin. "Yes."

"You were sent to find other wolves?"

"Not exactly, but yeah, sort of." He considers me for a moment, and I can read his thoughts clearly. He wants to tell me, but he's struggling with his sense of honor. Things are pretty black and white for this guy.

"You've already let me in on this much, you might as well tell me the whole story," I encourage.

"Foxfire's dad Johnny became part of a government research project on shifters. He died in captivity."

"What?" My mouth drops open with horror.

"They came after Foxfire two years ago when they figured out he had a child. Who knows, maybe they were interested in half-breed genetics. Those guys who trashed your Airstream weren't mafia. They were men looking to capture Foxfire."

Icy prickles race down my arms and up my spine. "But Tank protected her." I flip back to the memories from two years ago and see the pieces explode and rearrange.

"That's right. The packs have been searching out these labs and destroying them. We had word there might be one up this way so my alpha sent me on a fact-finding mission. To see if I could ferret anything out."

I generally try not to get too polarized over anything. Right and wrong, good and bad are all subjective, really. I want to be in allowance of all things. To be one with nature and the Universe.

But fuck that. These men killed a man I cared about and came after my child.

They're definitely wrong.

And the only right I see here is to do everything I can to help seek justice and rescue any other shifters who might be in danger.

I fold my fingers together and lean forward. "Okay, so what are we looking for?"

"We?"

I sit straighter. "That's right. These people killed the father of my child and tried to take her prisoner. Damn straight I'm going to help find them."

Titus nods. "I have to respect that. All right. Well, all the labs have been located in remote locations—government owned wilderness areas. The actual laboratories are concrete bunkers. They are inside fenced grounds with guard towers and security cameras.

Something about that sounds familiar. I've heard of a place like that in the Carson Forest. Who was telling me?

My eyes fly wide. "I've got it!" I stand up so quickly from the picnic table I hit the tops of my thighs on the wood. "Ouch."

"Slow down there, sunshine." Titus catches my casted elbow and steadies me. "What is it?"

"I had a date with this guy—"

Titus growls so loud it scares me. I mean, I know he would never hurt me, but my body reacts instinctively, freezing me in my tracks. The wound on my neck throbs.

"Stop it," I scold, recovering. "He was an idiot and I left early. You're not listening."

"Sorry." Titus shakes his head as if to recover his senses. He walks around the table, picks me up by the waist and lifts me away from the picnic table like I weigh nothing. "Tell me."

"Um… wow. I guess you have superhuman strength, too?"

"Yep. Go on."

I lick my lips, turned on by that show of strength and momentarily losing the thread of my thoughts. "Oh yeah—he was telling me how he got lost out in the Carson National Forest and he came upon this government looking building. He was sure they were housing aliens there. Government conspiracy crap. I thought he was a total nut-job and purged the whole story until now."

"Do you know where exactly?"

"No, but we could ask him. He works at the ski boot shop in town."

Titus' forehead wrinkles. "Who buys ski boots in the summer?"

I laugh. "Exactly! I don't know why they don't close for summer. I guess they sell enough t-shirts and other touristy stuff to make it work. Anyway, let's go!" I quickly stack our dishes and grab the tablecloth and flowers all in one armful.

Titus promptly removes everything from my hands and carries them inside. When I see him standing at my sink washing dishes, I want to jump him, but there's no time.

"Leave the dishes, wolf-man. Let's find this lab!"

Titus turns and frowns, looking down the length of my body. "I hate to complain, but I think clothes might be a good idea."

"Oh yeah!" I skitter past him and he slaps my ass, hard. "Ouch! That was shifter strength!" I toss over my shoulder as I head to the back of the Airstream to change.

"No it wasn't." There's laughter in his voice. "Baby, I would never use shifter strength on you."

"You just did!" I call out as I scramble into a pair of shorts and a halter top. "I mean outside. You picked me up."

"I mean I would never hurt you." He stomps down the center aisle, his brows drawn together like he's not sure if I know.

I place my hands—well, one full hand, one half-casted hand on his chest. "I know, wolf-man. I'm teasing. You should try it some time. Brighten… I mean, lighten up."

He's still frowning but he drops a kiss on the bridge of my nose. "I've got sunshine. I got all the light I need." He picks me up by the waist again, lifts me and sets me down on his other side.

"Now you're just showing off."

I love the low rumble of his chuckle. "You're onto me."

~

Titus

. . .

WE RIDE into town on the Harley, mainly because I need to keep Sunny's body close to mine. She wraps her arms around my waist and presses her chest against my back, humming softly. At least I think she's humming. It's hard to hear over the roar of the motor, but that's what it feels like. A soft reverberation that goes straight to my dick.

I've been riding a motorcycle since I was eight years old, but it's totally different with Sunny on the bike. She's a human. Fragile as fuck. One accident and she could be taken from me. I had the fear of that put into me with her crash earlier this week.

Not that I've ever had an accident in my life. My reflexes are sharp and my nerves steady. But I drive differently knowing I have precious cargo on the bike. Double-check my mirrors, keep my speed down.

I can't see Sunny but I sense her enjoyment and it does something to my wolf. He's content because she's content. It's crazy, but true. And there's no denying the euphoria I feel now that he's marked her. Like bubbles of joy that won't stop rising.

We swing by the bar where the dickwad works, but they aren't open yet, so we head to my place to shower and for me to change clothes. When I get out of the shower, I find fresh jars of flowers on the kitchen table, coffee table, end table and dresser.

I smile and shake my head with disbelief. Sunny. Bringing color to the world everywhere she goes. Crazy, wonderful woman.

I catch her around the waist and pull her in for a kiss. "Ready?"

She smiles up at me, looking more youthful than ever. I

guess good sex will do that to a woman. "Ready, big man. Let's go."

I put my huge helmet on her again and we ride over, even though it's not far. When we get in, I nearly choke when I see the douchebag she went out on a date with. Tall, skinny. Weaselly. Arrogant little prick. But it doesn't matter. He's not competition. She made that clear.

"Larry, hi!" She waves as we walk over. He's behind the bar shoveling ice into ice buckets.

"Oh, hey, Sunny." He gives me a wary glance.

Good. He definitely should know she's been claimed.

"Hey, we have a question for you."

It's surprising how grateful I am she said we not I.

"Remember that government building you ran across in the Carson Forest?"

He lights up, like this is a story he loves to tell. "The alien research site? Definitely. What about it?" He looks from Sunny to me with new interest.

"We'd like to ride out there on the bike and take a look around."

He shakes his head with authority. "No way you'll get in. I'm telling you, there are guard towers and guys with machine guns at the top. It's crazy secure." He looks like he wants to launch into his whole story, so I cut him short.

"Directions, man?"

"I don't think you want to go out there. It's the kind of place people don't come back from."

"You might be right about that," I say. "But yeah, we definitely want to go out. Can you give us directions?"

He leans forward on his forearms and launches into an avid description of how to get there. I can't stand when people give too much information in directions—it muddies the picture and makes it harder to remember the salient points. This guy's doing that. He describes every turn with great detail.

I grab the pen and order ticket book from his front pocket and plop them on the counter between us. "Draw a map," I command, using the timber of alpha command.

Lo and behold, it works. He shuts up and draws the map, like I ask. "You guys be careful. Hey—stop in here when you're back so I know you're safe. That way if they capture you, you can tell them that someone knows where you are and is going to go public if you don't get back." He looks immensely satisfied with himself and this solution, so I nod.

"Yeah, sure thing. Thanks." I wave the paper with the map.

"Bye, Larry," Sunny calls out cheerfully, and I'm not even a tiny bit jealous. There's no way that guy could be attractive to her.

Still, I slide an arm around her waist as we walk out, showing my claim on her.

Outside, at the bike, I catch Sunny's chin. "I don't think you should go."

"Fuck that. I'm in this, too. My daughter and her father were harmed by these guys. I require justice." She folds her arms across her chest and sticks her chin out. "Besides, we're just a couple of lovebirds out for a drive, right?" She says brightly. "I'm your best cover."

She has a point. But I hate the idea of bringing her close to danger. I'll just scout it out. If it's what this guy describes, we will leave and I will call home to Wolf Ridge for backup.

I plop the helmet on her head and swing a leg over the bike. "Climb on, baby. Let's see what we can find."

~

SUNNY

LARRY'S MAP was shit and it takes us nearly an hour and a half of backtracking to find the unmarked road he described, but eventually we do. Titus hides the Harley behind a boulder and we hike in on foot. He holds my hand and swings our arms together like we're on a picnic or date of some kind.

The hike is about a half mile in and then the road just seems to stop.

There's nothing here.

Titus turns around in a circle. "Wrong road?"

The hairs stand up on the back of my neck. "No," I murmur. "I sense evil here."

He raises his brows.

I'm used to people thinking I'm nuts when I say things like that, so I just shrug, but he scans the trees more closely. "From which direction?"

The pleasure of being believed does something fluttery to my chest. I close my eyes to feel the energy. It blasts me from straight ahead. I open my eyes and point. Definitely that way.

Titus moves in that direction without comment. We

walk into the woods, no path to follow, nothing. It doesn't make sense that a lab would be out here beyond the road. The kind of lab Larry described would require a large parking area with many cars. Not a dead end dirt road and a hike into a pathless forest.

I start to doubt my intuition. "Maybe I'm wrong. This doesn't make sense."

Titus shakes his head. "I don't think you're wrong." He turns to face me and starts stripping off his clothes.

"Oh! Okay." I wasn't really feeling the romance at this precise moment, but with Titus, I'm always down. His passion sets my body on fire. I start to pull off my own shirt and he freezes.

"What are you doing?" He's fully naked now, his muscled body like a work of art.

"Um…" I cock my head. "What are you doing?"

He throws back his head and lets out a booming laugh that makes all the birds in the trees scatter. "Oh, baby. I would love to nail you up against this tree right now, but I was going to shift and sniff around. I can smell better when I'm in wolf form."

Oh.

My face grows warm. "Right. Totally. Got it."

Titus saunters toward me, his dick at full salute. "Why'd you have to go and show me these?" He cups one of my small breasts and rubs his thumb over the nipple.

I squirm, already wet for him. "Titus, don't. *Go*!" I point toward the direction of the evil.

He chuckles again. "Rain check?" He brushes his lips across mine.

I groan. "Definitely."

"Stay here. Do not move." In a blur of motion, he changes to wolf form, his four paws huge in the dirt.

I watch in awe as he trots off, nose to the ground, following the scents. Beautiful creature. I'm struck for a moment with honor that he showed me his wolf. That he trusts me with his secret. That I get to be a part of this strange and private society he and my daughter inhabit. It's a privilege, for sure.

He disappears from sight and I wait, listening to the stirring of the forest around me. A few minutes later, I hear a whistle.

"Sunny! Come check this out." I hear Titus call.

I leave Titus' clothes and boots and jog in the direction of his voice. "Titus?"

"Over here."

I have to go around a huge boulder to find him—in all his naked glory—at the edge of a drop-off.

I gasp. Down below, hidden from aerial view by the natural outcropping of rocks, lies a concrete bunker. On the other side is the elevated guard tower and a different dirt road that leads to what appears to be an underground parking lot.

"This is it!" Titus' eyes gleam the bright blue of his wolf. His aura is a bold red-orange. He's ready for battle. "I don't see or hear anyone around but I'm going in closer. Stay here and keep an eye out, okay?"

"Be careful, Titus."

"I will." He shifts and lands on all fours, already in stride.

From my vantage point, I can watch him the whole

time. He skirts back and forth down the steep incline, leaping from rock to rock until he makes it to the bottom. There, he stays low, in the shadows, sniffing around the perimeter.

I wish I had a pair of binoculars. I can't be positive, but I don't think I see anyone in the guard tower.

I'm surprised to see Titus run right for what appears to be the front door. When he goes in, I charge down after him. No way I'm letting him go into that place alone.

I skid and slide down the mountainside, then slowly climb down the boulder face. It's not nearly as easy as Titus made it look. Before long, I'm literally rock climbing without a belay and it's scary as hell.

Rocks slide out beneath me and scatter to the ground far below, warning me I'm far too high to sustain a drop. I move one foot. A hand. Try to figure out the best way to go.

Fuck, this is totally impossible with my casted arm. I look back up the way I came.

Crap. I don't think I can even get back up that way. And I can't go down anymore. I whimper.

"Sunny!"

Relief pours through me at the sound of Titus' voice below. I don't dare turn to look though. I'm frozen, hanging on for dear life, my limbs trembling, my fingers slipping from sweat. "Sunny, look at me."

Slowly, slowly, I turn my head to look over my shoulder and down. Titus is right beneath me, about twenty-five feet. He's holding his arms out. He's still naked. I'm not sure I'm going to get used to that.

"Let go, baby. I'll catch you."

I don't even hesitate. I trust this man completely, and I'm definitely willing to accept his help. I let go and drop, squeaking as the wind rushes along my skin. I collide into Titus with a thud, but he drops his arms and his knees, swinging me around to break the fall. I wrap my arms around his neck and kiss his cheek.

"You saved me!" I breathe.

"I don't know about that," he says with a chuckle. "But what in the hell were you doing, little lady? I'm going to turn your ass pink for scaring the shit out of me."

I suck his earlobe between my lips and release it with a pop. "Promise?"

He eases me gently to my feet and pops my ass without any force at all. "Cute, baby. Very cute."

I turn around and look at the building and my eyes fly wide. There are no doors. In fact, it appears a bomb went off where the doors used to be. "What happened? Is the building empty?"

He nods. "Yeah, but this was definitely a shifter lab. I smell weird shifter smell all over the place."

"What's weird shifter scent?"

He takes my hand and leads me toward the building. "Unidentified animal. They were experimenting on turning humans into shifters. Genetic modification shit. Experiments didn't always work. There's these guys from a lab in California that are just... weird. One's an owl, I think. The other two—I'm not even sure. Some kind of canine?" he shakes his head. "It's fucking tragic."

"Oh my goddess."

"Yeah. It's a wonder they even know how to function

after what they've been through."

We stop at the entrance. "What do you think happened here?"

"It looks like this lab has already been taken out, but it wasn't by us. It was obviously by force, though."

"Yeah."

We enter into darkness, which doesn't seem to bother Titus in the least.

"Are you sure there's no one here?"

He squeezes my hand. "Positive. I thought you might want to have a look around, but we can go back out if you're scared. I'll come back later to really search and see if there are any more clues. From what I can tell, everything's been emptied and destroyed. There's no equipment, data, files, anything. It's just an empty, burned out bunker with cages and prison cells."

I shiver, the sense of desperation, terror and evil pulling at me from every corner. There are entities hanging around here—probably ghosts of the departed test subjects, but I'm too creeped out to acknowledge them to ask.

"Yeah, let's go back. I can't actually see anything anyway."

Titus stops. "Oh shit. Right. I'm sorry, baby. I forgot."

We retrace our steps, and I'm relieved when we step into the light.

Until I see three men in black step out with guns pointed right at us.

itus

A SNARL RIPS out of my throat, and I shift before I even have a chance to think. The need to protect Sunny is too great. My wolf body-checks her to shove her back behind me.

My brain isn't working yet—I'm in full fight-mode, ready to rip their throats out.

One of them laughs like he's going to enjoy killing me.

Another one steps forward. "*Shift, wolf.*" The words enter my body and reverberate through. There's alpha command in them. It gets my attention, even though I'm unwilling to obey.

It helps kick my brain back online.

Shifters.

These guys are shifters.

Which doesn't necessarily mean they are friendly. But

their scents are familiar. These are the wolves from Sunny's place.

"*Shift, wolf,*" he repeats.

I shift, calmer, now. A little more able to think. Still, I angle my body in front of Sunny's to shield her from them.

"What are you doing here?" the alpha demands.

I narrow my eyes, not sure how much to say.

Sunny steps out from behind me, hands on her hips. "We know what you're up to!" she asserts. "We know, and we're not the only ones. Experimenting on shifters. Kidnapping them. Tracking down their children. We're not going to let you get away with it."

The alpha raises an eyebrow.

"Sunny," I say in a low voice. "These guys are the wolves we saw outside your place last night."

"Oh." Her eyes widen and she steps back to my side. I drop an arm around her shoulders and pull her against me. "Well, what are they doing here, then?"

The alpha's lips twitch. He has black hair and the smooth dark skin of a Native American. One of the other men looks similar, like they're related. He's young for an alpha—early thirties, tops. "I asked you first."

"Point those weapons away from my female," I demand, even though I'm out-numbered and out-gunned. They're wolves. They should know a mated wolf will stop at nothing to protect his female and my mating mark scent is all over Sunny. Even if it means taking on three much younger and well-armed wolves.

The alpha gives a tiny nod and the guns drop. "Talk."

"I was sent to find intel on this lab. Our pack had word

132

there was still an operational lab in New Mexico. Apparently, it's already been shut down."

"Your pack sent an old wolf and a human female to take down a lab?" One of the guys asks derisively.

I lift my lip and growl in his direction.

"What do you know about labs like these?" the alpha asks.

I study the wolves a little more and grow uneasy. They may be shifters, but they hold themselves like military. Like Nash, the shifter from the lab outside San Diego. They have the stance of soldiers—shoulders back, chest up. Huge muscles bulging through their black t-shirts. The guns they're carrying don't look like civilian weapons, not that I really know much about guns. And they definitely know how to handle them. Not like thugs who bought themselves big guns on the black market. But like professionals who handle guns with respect and care.

Could these men be working for the government? Could they actually be part of this program? Maybe a result of it?

I narrow my eyes. "What do you know?" I counter.

He looks at me for a long time. "I know who dismantled this lab." His gaze meets mine squarely.

I relax. "You did?"

He gives a single nod.

"I know who took down labs just like it in California and Utah," I tell him.

Again, the quiet nod. "Your pack?"

"Extended pack, yes."

"So you know what they did here? This Data-X corporation?" He lifts his chin in the direction of the building.

133

"Unfortunately, yes. Were there… survivors?"

He considers me another long moment, as if still weighing whether he can trust me. "Yes. And they require placement. We can't keep them here safely long term. Taos is way too small."

I scrub a hand over my beard. "I will talk to my alpha, but I'm sure they can be accommodated in Arizona— either Tucson or Phoenix or both. There's plenty of room and employment if they're seeking asylum."

The alpha steps forward and extends his hand. "Rafe Lightfoot."

"Titus Brown. This is Sunny Hines. Her daughter's father was killed in one of the labs."

"I'm sorry for your loss," Rafe offers as he shakes her hand. To me, he says, "Check with your alpha. I'm not going to expose these shifters to anyone new unless I have assurances they will be given full assistance."

I nod my agreement and pull out my phone.

The shifter who mocked me earlier snorts and I quickly realize why. There's no cell phone coverage out here. Zero bars.

"Give me your phone number," I say to Rafe.

He doesn't move. His ability to remain perfectly still is unnerving. The one who I'm pretty sure must be his brother has the same mastery. "We'll rendezvous. Ramirez Bar at sixteen hundred hours."

If I had any doubt of their military background, it's gone. "Who are you guys?" I demand.

"We're nobody," he answers. "And I'll ask you to forget you ever met us when this is over."

I shrug. I can live with that. If they're some kind of

secret-ops organization that takes down government-funded atrocities, I'm not going to protest. "Sixteen hundred hours. Ramirez Bar."

"That's right. We can give you a lift back to your bike, seeing as how your female had some difficulty scaling the rocks."

He says it mildly, so I don't take offense, but then the shifter who's been an ass from the beginning says, "You might need to get your nose checked. You *do* know you marked a human, right?"

I don't think. I just growl and launch myself at him, but the two others catch me and pull me back. They're strong enough to hold me, but I struggle until Sunny slips around the front of me and puts her palm on my chest. My wolf instantly calms.

"Don't mind Deke," Rafe murmurs. "He's always spoiling for a fight."

Deke's laugh is slightly maniacal. Okay, the guy's got a screw or two loose. Not my problem.

I ease up and they release me.

"Mention my female again and you're dead," I warn him.

He grins from ear to ear and fucking winks.

Crazy bastard.

Sunny's still got her hand on my chest, pushing me back, so I shift my focus to her. Where I want it to be, anyway.

The other man holds out his hand. "Lance, I'm Rafe's brother." Another shifter of few words.

I shake it and nod. Sunny offers hers with that wide smile. Neither of us offer a handshake to Deke.

We walk out to a vehicle that probably cost as much as a small house. It's the Mercedes version of a Hummer. I want to hate it, but I have to admit, it's pretty sweet.

"Here, man, I don't want your bare ass on my seats." Deke tosses a towel at me and I wrap it around my waist.

They drive us up and out of the mini gorge and loop around to the dead-end road where we left the Harley, my clothes just a short hike away.

"See you tonight," I say as I climb out and hold Sunny's hand to help her down.

"Yep."

CHAPTER 9

 *unny*

I LEAN MY HELMET AGAINST TITUS' back and review what just happened.

Hearing the jabs that jerk took at Titus over me has me mad. Not for myself, but on Titus' behalf. No wonder he's felt so *unavailable* to me. My instincts weren't wrong. We are literally a separate species.

And his own kind mocked him for being with me.

Maybe, as much as we're attracted to each other and as much as we care about each other, a relationship is impossible.

I don't want to think about that now, though, so I push it out of my mind. Titus is still here on a job, and I intend to help him with it. After that, we can talk.

We ride back to Titus' place and he calls his alpha to

report. I'm not trying to eavesdrop, but I notice he's only saying *I*.

Not *we*.

He hasn't mentioned my involvement at all.

Would he get in trouble?

Or is this more like... embarrassment? Like we're in high school and it's not cool to hang out with the weirdo.

The girl I tried really hard not to be in high school so I could catch the heart and hand of Jack.

Are we like a biracial couple one hundred years ago where he likes me in private but doesn't want to be seen with me in public?

I'm not down with that. It took me a while, but I've embraced who I am. I don't want to be with anyone who isn't cool with the whole package. Human genes and all.

But when Titus gets off the phone and wraps a beefy arm around me from the back to kiss my neck, I melt.

Just a little longer. I'm not ready to move on from him yet. The sex is too good. Feeling cared for and protected, too delicious.

I'll stick with my plan of riding this thing out.

"My alpha offered to take them all in," Titus says, lips still at my neck. "I'm going to hire a bus to take them all to Arizona if they want to go. Want to come along? You could stop in Tucson to visit the kids?"

It's not because I'm not ready for this to be over that I say *yes*.

Not at all.

And I am always excited to see Foxfire. I give her a call to tell her the news. Although not revealing what I know about her is going to kill me.

"Hi, Sunny!" She picks up.

"Foxfire, darling! How are you?"

"I'm good. How are you feeling?"

"Much better, darling. My bruises are fading and the arm doesn't hurt a bit anymore. Titus is taking good care of me."

"So he's still with you?"

"Yes, he's still here. And I'm going to head back to Arizona with him when he leaves in the next couple of days. I want to see you two."

"Sounds good, Sunny. I have some good news for you, too."

I gasp, my heart somersaulting. "Oh, goddess are you pregnant?"

"No, no, no, no, no. Sunny, no. I told you we're not even trying. But it is about a baby."

"What baby?"

"Remember Jordy, my dad's sister from Utah?"

"Yes, of course. I never met her in person, but I remember Johnny talking about her." I gasp again, catching up. "Is she pregnant?" I can't help it, I get excited about babies even when it's someone I only met once who lives in Utah.

Foxfire laughs. "Yes, actually! Turns out, she ended up in Tucson. She mated—I mean married this big guy named Grizz and they're expecting their first baby."

"Oh goddess, that's wonderful! I want to see them when I'm there. Maybe we can arrange a shower for her? I mean, we are her family, after all."

"I bet she'd love that, Sunny. I'll see if I can throw

something together last minute. When exactly are you getting here?"

"I'm not sure, but I'll let you know. In the next couple of days, I imagine. Titus is making arrangements."

It literally kills me not to tell her everything that's going on. I'm a terrible secret-keeper. But Titus' secrets are important to me, so I have to honor him.

"Great, Sunny. Can't wait to see you."

"Me neither, darling. Bye!"

I hang up and beam at Titus, who is looking at me quizzically. "My daughter's aunt is in Tucson now with a guy named Grizz and they're expecting a baby!"

Titus' smile is totally indulgent. He drops a kiss on the top of my head. "That's great, sunshine. I know you love those babies."

I snuggle against him and lean my head on his chest. Try to ignore how right it feels.

Titus

SUNNY AND I meet the Taos wolves at the appointed time and place.

"Hi, guys!" Sunny beams that bright smile and waves from the doorway.

Four of them sit at a table in the back corner, sharing a couple pitchers of beer. It's the same three from earlier today and one more who also appears military-trained.

They look over. Rafe barely acknowledges us with a slight lift of his chin.

"Hey," she tries again when we sit down. She leans across the table and sticks out her hand to the guy we don't know. "I'm Sunny."

He's younger than the others, probably late twenties, with Captain America good-looks. "Channing." His dimpled smile is just as bright as Sunny's.

A low growl starts in my throat when he takes her hand and he immediately yanks it back. "No offense, silver."

At first I think he's referring to my beard, but then I realize he was the fourth wolf out during the full moon.

Normally after a wolf marks his mate, the extreme possessiveness and jealousy eases. I don't know why mine seems even worse. Probably because despite my wolf's claim, I haven't figured out how to keep her.

Rafe pushes the beer and two empty glasses our way without a word.

Quiet fellow.

Once again I'm struck by the stillness he embodies. I follow suit and don't speak, pouring a glass of beer for myself and Sunny and taking a long sip.

"Well?" Rafe says.

"We'll take them all. No problem. I'll take care of transport."

Rafe cocks his head. "You don't know how many there are."

"Doesn't matter. Alpha Green will figure it out. His son owns nightclubs and real estate all over Tucson, and the pack owns a brewery north of Phoenix. We can find jobs for them. Get them integrated. Help with the PTSD."

Lance gives a solemn nod. "Good. You have an under-standing of what they're dealing with."

"I know a few from the California lab. They func-tion... but barely. Real paranoid and jittery. Definitely off." I think of Declan, Laurie and Parker and shake my head. They are definitely unique characters.

"Good," Lance repeats.

"We have two dozen refugees," Rafe tells me. We took them in six weeks ago when we located the lab and took it down. They are currently camped nearby."

"Two dozen. Okay. I can hire a bus to take them down to Phoenix."

Rafe nods.

When I realize we're back to silence, I decide to try to get some of my questions answered. "So do you guys work for the government?"

"Contractors for hire. Former active military. The order to shut down that lab came from the government, though."

Sunny and I glance at each other, digesting that news.

"Yeah, if we'd known such a thing existed when we were in the forces, we probably would've all defected, right then and there," Channing offers. Clearly he's the only talkative one in the group. "Because what we found in that lab was wrong."

All four of them nod, a haunted quality sneaking into their sharp gazes.

"All wrong," Deke agrees, and throws back his beer, draining a full glass in a few gulps.

"So why did the government send you in to shut it down forcibly, if it was their lab to begin with?" Sunny asks.

Rafe shakes his head. "They didn't brief us much, but from what I understand, it was a joint-venture project between government and private industry."

"Data-X," I concur.

"Right. The major players in Data-X were eliminated. I'm guessing by your network."

I nod.

"The government chose to close the project and eliminate any evidence of what remained."

A chill runs up my spine. Are these guys government assassins?

Not wanting to know one way or the other, I down my beer and stand up. "I'll arrange the bus. When can we meet the refugees?"

"Let us know when you book the bus and we'll give you the location," Rafe says.

I barely manage not to roll my eyes at their cloak and dagger shit. "This time can I at least get a phone number?"

"Yes." Rafe turns on his phone.

I pull mine out and it beeps with a message.

"That's me," he says.

I don't even bother asking how he got my number. These guys probably already know everything there is to know about me, Sunny, and my pack.

Sunny isn't deterred by their reticence. "So what's the scoop—were you guys, like, special ops?"

All four of them consider her, which tells me she hit the mark. Her intuition is always spot on.

"Shifter ops," Channing grins and takes a sip of beer.

Sunny's eyes light up and she leans forward. "You were all like, shifter CIA? Navy SEALS? Special Forces?"

"Something like that," Rafe mumbles.

"And now that you're retired, you're a pack?" she asks brightly.

"Something like that," Deke answers.

"We're a company—Black Wolf Security," Channing offers.

The other three look at him.

"What? It's not a secret."

"Need to know," Deke sing-songs.

"We're a legit company. Rafe bought a *headquarters*."

"Still," Rafe says. "Low profile."

Low profile, minimal words. I'm getting the essence of these guys. And while I think they're the good guys, I'm also certain danger surrounds them. And my wolf doesn't like Sunny near danger.

I stand up and help Sunny out of her chair. "I'll be in touch, then."

Rafe nods. Channing lifts his glass. Deke and Lance remain still.

I shake my head as we leave. Not sure I've met a stranger shifter pack since those crazy three moved over from California.

And they had good reason.

Of course, these guys probably do, too, but I doubt I want to know what it is.

CHAPTER 10

S unny

I TUCK a bottle of wine and an opener in my picnic basket, along with our lunch and climb in the bus to meet Titus at his place. It's our last afternoon in Taos before we head to Phoenix with the refugees, and I intend to make the most of it.

I've been ignoring the little niggles of anxiety that have been running through me as our end draws ever closer.

I don't want to think about it. Don't want to give him up. Being with Titus feels too good.

Too right.

And every time I'm with him, his auric field turns pink.

He loves me.

He hasn't said it, but it's clear.

And I feel the same way.

I find him sitting outside his place, waiting for me. He surges to his feet as soon as I pull up.

"Hey, big man," I call as I jump out and hoist the picnic basket.

"What's this?" He takes it from me. I didn't tell him our plans, just that I wanted to show him something this afternoon.

I beam up at his handsome face. "We're going to have a picnic at the waterfall," I tell him.

"There's a waterfall?"

"Yep. And we're going there. On your bike," I say. "It will be easier and way more fun." The road up to the waterfall gets a little rough.

Titus gives me a lopsided grin. It's like smiling is an unfamiliar act for him and his mouth is still remembering how it works. "Sounds good to me." He straps the picnic basket onto the back of the bike and we climb on. I give him directions and hum softly as his bike travels up through the trees on a rugged dirt road.

Eventually, we get to the gate, where he parks and takes the picnic basket. "Not much farther," I promise. "A tiny hike."

"You can't scare me with a hike," Titus says with a laugh. "No need to sell it." He takes my hand.

I look up at him, admiring the halo of pink and gold around him. The happiness in the lines of his face. He seems changed since he came here last week, and I know it's because of me.

Because of us.

So isn't that enough for me? Can I let myself have this happiness, a real, lasting relationship for once?

The joy bubbling in my chest says yes.

"So what's in this basket anyway?" Titus hoists it on his shoulders and takes my hand.

"I'm glad you asked. I know wolves are carnivores, but you're also human, so all that meat can't be good for your health. So everything I packed is vegan!" I give him a bright Sunny smile.

"Woman," he growls.

"I'm kidding. I packed meat. Lots and lots of meat. But I did make vegan muffins, and you have to eat one."

He grunts.

"Titus," I scamper ahead to stand on a rock and face him. When we're eye-to-eye, I tell him soberly, "You will love the taste of my muffin."

He shakes his head.

"What?" I ask, even though I know he's going to roll his eyes at me for being crazy.

"You are too cute," he says, and when I blink, he tugs me close for a kiss. "I will eat the hell out of your muffin," he promises. Shiver.

We follow the stream up until we hit the rock face with the water tumbling down. Sometimes it's no more than a trickle, but we had a huge snow season this year, so the water level is still super high.

"Beautiful," Titus murmurs.

"Right?" I tug him up to the top of a boulder where we open the picnic basket and he pops the cork on the bottle of wine and pours it into the two small mason jars I stuck in.

"Cheers," he says softly, lifting his glass to me.

"Here's to…" I stop and swallow. I want to say, *to us*. Or to *second chances*. But what if this is actually a goodbye toast?

"To future possibilities." He meets my gaze squarely and holds it like he's trying to tell me something. Like he wants to explore our future possibilities.

I want that too.

"To future possibilities." I clink his glass. "With you." The last part is barely a whisper but he hears it. He probably has superhuman hearing, too. He catches behind my neck and pulls me in for one of those possessive kisses. The kind that consumes me, sets me on fire, turns me inside out. His tongue's in my mouth, fingers stroking between my legs.

I moan.

He pulls me onto him, straddling his lap in a seated position. One hand crushes my breast, the other still holds my head captive. All the while, his lips move over mine with that passion he always brings.

I'm already wet for him. Already eager. I pull my tank top off and he growls, eyes glowing bright blue.

He looks around with a ferocity, like if there's anyone around and they saw me, he's going to rip them limb from limb.

"We're alone, Titus," I murmur. "Hardly anyone knows about this place."

"Wanna ride Spartacus, angel?" He yanks my hips over the hard bulge in his pants.

I make a purring sound. "Give him to me, big guy."

He groans and frees his erection as I stand and drop my

shorts. I'm totally naked out in nature—one of my favorite things. And with the man I love.

Goddess, is it true?

It totally is. I love Titus.

With that joyful thought, I straddle my man again and drop down, sinking onto his erection.

We both groan with the pleasure of it. He's too big— he's always too big, but the stretch is so wonderful.

He lets me control the show as I get comfortable and do my best to hang onto his shoulder with my good arm. Then he grips my bare ass and takes charge. He pulls me up over his cock and back down in a beautiful, rhythmic motion. A circular motion that makes me dizzy with pleasure.

"Yes, Titus," I encourage.

As if this guy ever needs encouragement.

But we surf the wave together, eyes locked on each other's in some kind of tantric meditation. Time stops. The waterfall stops. There's nothing but our two hearts beating together, our two bodies blending and coming apart in perfect communion.

"*This,*" I murmur in awe.

"What, baby?"

"Nirvana," I gasp.

We found it. The highest state of consciousness. Of ecstasy. Of pleasure.

Titus grips my ass harder, fingers digging into the flesh. He gives my cheek a slap.

Time starts again. Or I should say the time bomb starts ticking.

Need licks through me like flames.

I have to come.

Now.

"Sunny," Titus grates. His voice is beyond rough. His expression pained.

"Ready?" I gasp.

"Fuck, yeah." He pulls me down harder, jacks up to meet me. I'm bouncing on his lap, my small breasts jiggling, my breath cut short with each magical thrust.

"Please," I whine, even though I know it's coming.

"Fates, yeah," he shouts.

I bounce higher. My eyelids flutter as I lose the ability to focus. To breathe. To remember my name.

And then we both come. My screams mingle with his roar, echoing off the canyon walls and coming back to us as the reverberation of our climax echoes through our bodies.

When we stop moving, I collapse against him, into his arms, my head on his shoulder, unable to even keep my own head up.

When my consciousness returns, Titus is rocking me slowly from side to side, murmuring, "Beautiful female. Wonderful, magical female."

My heart feels like it will burst wide.

And then I know with total certainty—

I am loved back.

CHAPTER 11

itus

WE MEET the charter bus and the shifter refugees the next morning in a dirt parking lot at the juncture of three highways. The black wolf pack show up in two Humvees and Deke's Mercedes G63. Whatever their jobs really are or were, they have plenty of money.

The refugees climb out of the vehicles. Even though they've been free for six weeks now, they still wear shell-shocked, wary expressions. I catch their strange, mixed scents—a jumble of animals, nothing that makes sense. It's just like the misfit shifters from California. Alpha Green asked those three to come up to Wolf Ridge and meet the bus, so these new refugees will have shifter's who have been through what they have to advocate for them and help build trust.

"We're going to provide escort to Arizona," Rafe tells me. "Make sure you arrive safe."

I shake his hand. "Thank you."

A young female walks up with a baby bunny cupped in one hand. Her head is bent, her soft dark 'fro making a halo around her face, and she's murmuring softly to the animal.

"Oh how sweet!" Sunny chirps. "Is it hurt?"

The female looks up in surprise, then ducks her head again. Her warm brown skin glows as she cuddles the creature. I get the Disney princess reference. No one would blink if she burst into song. "No. I'm just saying goodbye."

Sunny smiles as if this is the most normal thing in the world.

"Hope you don't mind animals," Rafe mutters. "Allison made friends with just about every creature in the area. Even prey animals were hanging around our door." He shakes his head but an underlying gentleness and affection shows through. Like he really got to know and appreciate these shifters.

The last of my reservations about him disappear.

"Fuck, Allie, you gonna bring the menagerie?" A short, pale female shifter with a nose ring and a mohawk of black hair stalks up. She crosses tautly muscled arms over her chest and sunlight flashes on the huge skinning knife she's carrying.

I step between her and Sunny.

"Don't be silly, Fiona," Allison says, and puts the wild rabbit down. "Go on," she encourages until it hops off. Allison heads over to Fiona, and hugs her side, laying her head on the tiny goth woman's shoulder, ignoring the knife.

"Thank fuck," Fiona says fondly, winding her free arm around Allison's shoulders. "They like you, but whenever they got close to me they peed themselves. I'll buy you a stuffed animal at the gas station."

Rafe clears his throat. "Who says you're allowed off the bus when we stop for gas?"

"Deke, actually." Fiona tosses her chin in the direction of the crazy wolf. "I told him Allison would cry if she didn't get a Taos key chain. He promised."

"Sure he did."

"Oh, Rafe, please," Allison coos.

Rafe rolls his eyes. "Fine. Get you off my back."

Fiona points her knife at him. "You're gonna miss us. Admit it."

I clear my throat as Rafe shakes his head. "Time to get on the bus. Load up!"

"You gonna be okay, baby?" I steer Sunny to her VW.

"Of course," she goes up on tip-toe to kiss me on the nose. So fucking cute. I hook her close and claim her mouth.

An "oooOOOoooo" chorus goes up from the peanut gallery. I give them the finger and Allison and Fiona both cackle.

"Until later." Sunny gives me her signature smile and climbs in the bus. I follow her on my bike, swallowing down my own sense of foreboding.

Sunny and I still haven't spoken about the future.

About what happens after we get to Arizona.

All I know is I don't want to say goodbye to her. My wolf probably won't let me.

But I also can't figure out how to keep her either. Even if she were the type to settle down—which she isn't, thanks to her asshole ex-husband—I can't exactly bring her into my pack. It's forbidden.

So where does that leave us? Me trying to convince her long-term relationships can work? It would have to be away from the pack. Maybe moving into her Airstream, hoping that as long as we stay mobile and tour the arts and crafts scene, she won't feel pinned down?

That's crazy, though. I don't even fit in that Airstream. It creaks every time I set foot in it. I have to duck to walk. And I'd probably go nuts.

But you'd be with Sunny, my wolf argues.

True. Very true.

I resolve to talk to her about it when we get to Wolf Ridge. After my mission is complete.

Sunny

THE DRIVE from Taos to Phoenix is hot. Mountains melt into desert and the air outside grows increasingly more stifling. We pass through Navajo land. I keep catching myself gnawing my lip.

It'll be fine. I release my chokehold on the steering wheel. *I'm just meeting Titus' entire pack. No biggie.*

But by the time we pull into the parking lot of Wolf

Ridge Rec Center, the concrete in my stomach has settled in to stay. *Calm down.* I jump out of my bus to assist my new shifter friends.

Fiona is already off the bus, a pitifully small bag slung over her shoulder. These shifters had nothing. Not even clothes to wear, if Fiona's makeshift outfit is anything to go by. She looks like she cut up a big man's t-shirt and a pair of running shorts to fit her. *That's right, focus on helping.*

When Allison steps off the bus, she stumbles. A lanky male catches her, his cheeks flushing as they both straighten. When Allison thanks him, he flushes and stammers, "W-w-welcome."

"You're sweet," Allison tells him and his thick glasses steam. His ears practically combust. "I'm Allison."

"I'm Laurie," says the tall male.

"Allie, quit flirting," Fiona says. "I need the little puppies room."

Allison blushes.

"I'll show ya where it is." A dark-haired guy steps up, flashing white teeth.

Fiona's head snaps around. "You're Irish," she accuses.

"That's right. Name's Declan." He puts his hands up like she's threatened him. She's still holding the long knife, so she might. "Pleased to meet ya. And might I say, ya are the most beautiful shifter I've ever seen."

Fiona narrows her eyes him. She points the knife. "Back off, whiskey dick."

"All right, all right." He retreats, muttering something about a "fecking violent leprechaun."

"I see you're making friends," I tease Fiona.

"What? Oh, he'll be fine." But Fiona scowls in Declan's direction. "I was just messing with him."

"He's cute," Allison says. "Not my type," she pets the tall, gangly guy beside her. "But you two looked good together."

"And I thought I was a matchmaker," I say. "You called that pretty quick."

"When Fiona likes someone she picks a fight," Allison informs us. "It's a test."

"I see. To me, it looked like you wouldn't touch his ten-foot pole," I joke. Everyone's eyes widen and I realize what I said. "I mean"—I wave my hands wishing I could rewind thirty seconds—"you wouldn't touch *him* with a ten-foot pole."

"I was gonna say, ten feet? Damn, woman." Fiona whistles. "Maybe I will go after him."

"Mhhmmm." Allison turns to me. "Sunny, do you have that willow bark? I know I'm a shifter, but I get these headaches."

"I get headaches too," Laurie murmurs, blinking at Allison. He looks like he's seen an angel.

"I have the willow bark in my bus," I say. "I'll get it."

Allison thanks me and shoots Laurie a smile that rocks him back on his feet.

Do all shifters pair up this fast? I guess when you find your mate, that's it.

A prickle in my shoulder makes me cover the bite Titus gave me with my hand. I've never had a man be so rough in the bedroom, but I love it. The marks are healing nicely, but I'll make him rub calendula or arnica cream on it later. Maybe both.

I'm rummaging around in my herb closet when Titus' voice rumbles through the walls. I twitch aside the curtain. The window badly needs washing, but Titus' bulk is recognizable. He's talking to another big guy in slacks and a button-down and he looks tense.

Titus grew silent and remote the last leg of the journey. My gut says it's over me. Us.

Is he worried about this being the end for us? I'm starting to feel like it doesn't have to be. We still have the trip down to Tucson together. And what if... what if we could stick together a while longer? I don't know how, but damn, it seems like for the first time, there's a man worth giving up my independence for. Giving my trust and heart to.

Titus

FUCK. I noticed the nasty glance Alpha Green sent my way when he saw Sunny's bus. I don't know why I didn't include her in any of my reports.

Yes I do.

I was a fucking coward, that's why.

So here I am again. Letting a female blind me to my responsibilities to my pack. I could lose everything again, here.

"Interesting friends you made up there," he remarks, his eyes traveling not to the refugees, but to the black wolf pack. Of course, I can't help but wonder if he's also talking about Sunny.

"Yes. They play it close to the chest. I believe they can be trusted, but it took a long time to get a read on them."

"So they're mercenaries, basically. Dangerous jobs for hire? Did you get the feeling they'd be sticking around up there?"

"I believe so, but they never revealed the location of their compound. I heard from one of the females that Lightfoot and his brother are from that area originally, but they joined the military right out of high school and haven't been back until now."

"And the human?" Alpha Green spits the word *human* as if he's talking about dog shit on his lawn.

My wolf nearly lets out a growl.

Fuck. I need to get it under control. I'm talking to my *Alpha*. The most important person in my sphere. I cannot allow my irrationality when it comes to females affect me.

"What is she doing here?"

"She, ah, got caught up in things."

"She knows about us." Green's voice is flat. Not a question. I can't deny the truth. I may avoid certain topics, but I'm not a liar. Especially not to an alpha.

"Her daughter is a fox shifter. Of course Sunny figured things out." It's mostly true. She had it half-figured out before I nearly turned moon-mad and bit her.

"I mean, she knows about *us*, specifically. This pack. You should've asked for permission to bring a human into Wolf Ridge. To our private compound. This isn't like you, Titus. I expect more."

I'm hit by a wave of nausea—a visceral reaction to the

condemnation of my alpha. All the memories of being called before the council of my previous pack. Receiving their physical attack, and then the more debilitating one of banishment come flashing back. My shame. My inadequacies as a father to protect my only pup. Losing my faith in my own ability to make good decisions.

Now I'm in the same place again.

"I guarantee she won't talk. Her daughter's part of the Tucson pack. She's pack family. But I'll get rid of her," I hear myself say. My own voice sounds like it's coming from a hundred miles away. Thin and empty. "No problem."

"You sure? Because I saw that mark on her neck." Green's eyes narrow. He's studying my face, and I can't seem to school my features. I don't even know what to show. What to say.

All the while, I'm fighting my wolf, who is howling, fucking howling inside at this betrayal of our mate.

I try to answer but my mind is blank. My tongue ten sizes too big.

"You have something to tell me?"

I shake my head dumbly. "Uh... no. We had a fling. The moon was full and I lost control, but it didn't mean anything. It doesn't mean anything."

Now I'm really going to puke. It's like I just tore my wolf from my humanity. Separated the two parts of myself that have always been in harmony. Heat and cold flush through my body. My organs twist and shiver.

"She's a human, like you said." My lips are somehow still moving even though I'm about to pass out. "And she doesn't stick around."

~

Sunny

What? I stagger back from the window, my hand on my chest. *I'll get rid of her.* Shot to the heart. Hurts worse than a bullet. After everything we shared together, I can't believe Titus would dismiss us so quickly.

It didn't mean anything.

Right. There is no *us.* I was a fool to think a guy with that many issues could commit.

Alpha Green says something I don't catch. I'm too busy pressing my palm against my aching chest, breathing hard. This is just like Jack all over again. I've been deemed unworthy by my faulty biology. Not good enough.

But the pain I'm feeling is my own fault. I did it. I let him in, and this is how it feels.

Like dying.

"I'm committed to the pack," Titus says. Of course he does. This is why he can't commit to me. Not that I ever asked him to. Not that we had any kind of committed relationship at all.

But still. Being summarily dismissed as a lowly human he has to get rid of goes straight to my sorest spot.

I don't stay to hear any more. I blunder back to the charter bus, where Fiona has invited Declan back, only to berate him more about his accent. I feel Titus coming over, so I insert myself into their group and lean towards Allison.

"Sorry." My voice comes out thick. "I don't have any willow bark after all."

Fiona frowns. "Sunny, are you okay?"

"Don't mind me," I wave my hand dismissively. "Long day."

"Real grateful to you boys—" Titus' voice booms and I fall silent. He's a few yards away, shaking Rafe's hand.

I want to be anywhere but here. I will myself invisible.

Allison steps forward, her face shining. For a second it looks like she's going to give the big military man a hug. "We just wanted to thank you—"

"No problem," Rafe cuts her off, retreating before she can touch him. His guys are already loaded up in their Humvees. Deke's G63 kicks up dust as he speeds off.

Right. Wolves don't like associating outside of their pack.

Rafe lowers mirrored shades, nods to Titus and Alpha Green before leaping into his brother's Humvee.

"Bye-bye, black wolves," Allison murmurs. She doesn't seem too upset at Rafe's stand-offishness.

I inch around to the outskirts of the group.

"All right, everyone," Alpha Green booms. "We've got sandwiches and drinks inside, and a bunch of my pack are figuring out places you can stay. And as soon as we can, we'll get information from everyone to reconnect you with your families and get you settled, wherever you want to go."

Shifters start drifting in the direction Alpha Green pointed.

"Titus"—Alpha Green waves—"gonna need you inside."

"Coming." Titus pivots in place, searching the crowd. His face is pale and drawn. Aura a brown-gray.

I shrink behind the bus. My hands are clammy, my head swims with the start of a killer migraine. He's looking for me. Of course, he could scent me out if he wanted, but after a few seconds he shrugs and heads inside the building. Almost everyone is gone.

"I'll get you some aspirin," Laurie tells Allison, offering his hand. She takes it and Laurie puffs up to his full height. Declan and Fiona head inside, Fiona's lip curled in a sneer as she banters with him.

Palming my keys, I get into my bus. Better to slip out now, before anyone notices. I need to get out of Wolf Ridge. Away from Titus.

He doesn't want me.

The cold thought keeps me going the full two and a half hours until I pull into the driveway outside my daughter's house.

Voices murmur inside. I knock.

A second later, my daughter's bright head fills the doorway. "Mom?" When she sees my face, her eyebrows pinch in worry under the mermaid colors of her hair.

Then and only then do I let my face crumple and begin to cry.

itus

THE HEAVINESS of my lies to Alpha Green coat my mouth.
I keep trying to tell myself it was for Sunny's own good.
To keep Alpha Green from worrying about her, or possibly
asking me to get her mind wiped by a vampire.

Bullshit.

I don't even need my wolf to snarl it at me. I know it
myself.

It was total self-preservation.

I didn't want to get kicked out of the pack over a
female again, so I acted like a coward.

But it's okay, if I can just get out of here, I'll find
Sunny and we can talk about our future. If she agrees to let
me be a part of her life, I can deal with Green then.

Even that doesn't mollify my wolf or me. I have a

current of uneasiness running through me at a mounting level.

To make it even worse, I can't spot Sunny anywhere. I haven't seen her for a couple hours now—not since we came inside, and she hasn't answered my text asking where she is.

Of course, Green's eye is on me the whole fucking time, so I haven't been able to shirk my duties and go find her, either.

At long last, I finish debriefing the pack council.

"Good work, everyone," Alpha Green congratulates the room. We interviewed a few of the shifters and conferenced in the tech guru Jackson King and his wife Kylie, a shifter with amazing hacking abilities. They're working on contacting the pack or family of each of the stolen shifters —those who want to go back. If the shifters prefer not to return to their homes, we'll help them settle. In the meantime, the Phoenix pack will continue to host everyone.

I give a vague nod when Pierce, one of my council buddies, claps me on the shoulder. "Good work, Titus."

"Yeah, thanks. I gotta get going, though. I'll see you all later."

I tried to get out of the meeting early a few times, but every time my Alpha would shoot me another question.

Sunny's a big girl. She can handle herself. Or so I keep telling my wolf. But nothing feels right about this.

In the main hall, only half the new shifters remain, helping clean up dinner or perusing the tables in the back covered with donated clothes and toiletries. The rest of the new shifters have been picked up by pack members who offered places to stay in their homes.

Allison and Fiona are still here, sitting with the two strange shifters from Tucson. I pause at the end of their table

"Where's Sunny?"

Allison frowns, exchanging a look with Fiona. "I haven't seen her in a while."

"Yeah, she didn't eat with us. Last I saw her was outside by her VW."

"Thanks." I head outside, an inexplicable sense of dread twisting in my gut.

"Sunny?" The low-slung sun slants into my eyes and I shade them, heading around the bus and SUVs, searching for the familiar silver flash. Amid the sea of smells, Sunny's fruit and herb scent teases me. I stride to the end of the parking lot. Where did she go? Did she pull around to the front of the building for some reason?

My wolf snarls insults at me and I ignore him. Not now. I gotta find Sunny. I need to get this shit figured out with her. Right away. Either we're together, or we're not. But I gotta know.

My wolf howls. *Mine. Our mate.*

I rub the back of my neck. I really gotta figure this situation out. I care for Sunny but I belong with my pack.

I blow out a breath and stare at the ground, my wolf tugging at my attention. It takes me a moment to under-stand what I'm seeing: a set of tire tracks curving through the dust.

Fuck. I guess this means we're not going to be together.

She left me.

Again.

~

SUNNY

FOXFIRE FILLS my mug with chamomile tea. Behind her, Tank takes up all the available space in the kitchen, leaning against the cabinets. His big form is so like Titus', it hurts to look in his direction.

"So you just left?" my daughter asks softly. She's calm but her colorful aura pulses with alarm. It's not everyday I surprise her on her doorstep and burst into tears.

"Yes." I wipe my eyes. "I didn't want to stay where I wasn't wanted. Given the choice between me and his pack, who is he going to choose?" I try to scoff. The bite on my shoulder throbs and I rub it with my palm. The pain radiates through my arm. "Do you have any arnica?" I tug on my collar.

Foxfire sucks in a breath, grabs my shirt and stares at the enormous hickey. "What the hell? Did Titus do this?"

"It's all right, darling." I push away her hand and cover the mark again. "Just a love bite." A big one.

"That's not a love bite. That's a mating mark."

I blink at her serious tone. "What?"

"Tank?" my daughter calls. Her man is already standing over me. "Let him see."

With a sigh, I drop my hand. His gaze zeroes in on the mark.

"It's nothing," I insist.

"It's not nothing. See?" Foxfire tugs away her own shirt and shows me a healed bite. "It's a wolf thing. They do it when they want to claim you. If Titus did that it means you're his mate."

"But... I'm human."

"Doesn't matter. His wolf claimed you as his."

"And then Titus renounced me. He called what we had 'a fling' and told his alpha it didn't mean anything." The words stab my heart all over again.

"Fuck," Tank mutters, and stomps off. The act is so Titus, tears fill my eyes.

"It's okay, Sunny." Foxfire covers my hand. "I promise, it'll be okay."

Titus

SHE LEFT. She fucking left.

I try to call her all the names I called my ex-wife. *Bitch. Traitor.* But my wolf doesn't want to play. He was glad to be rid of my ex wife, who lied to us from the beginning. Sunny didn't lie. She was true to herself, every day, and let me in knowing I might judge her.

I bring my phone to my ear before I realize it's buzzing.

Junior the screen reads. I answer. "Tank? Everything all right?"

"Nope. Gotta situation."

My heart falls to my boots. "Is it Foxfire? Did someone come for her?" Shit, I knew there'd be blowback. Didn't realize it would be so soon.

"Not Foxfire. She and I are fine. It's Sunny."

The world spins. "Sunny? She… she's there?"

"Yep. Turned up a half an hour ago, crying her eyes out. Apparently she heard you denounce her to Alpha Green."

The pieces rearrange and snap into place. My mind spins. What did I say to Green? Oh fates, it was bad. Really bad. "Fuck."

"Yeah."

"Tank, I—"

"You marked her, Dad. I saw the bite."

I can't speak.

"Listen, you can't put pack above your personal happiness. Pack isn't everything. And Sunny—she's not Mom. Not every female is like that."

It hurts, hearing Tank bring up his mother. He never talks about her if he can help it. I'd rather take a bullet than make my son remember the female who abandoned him.

"I know."

"Sunny isn't like that. She's loving and loyal."

"She left," I remind him. "Twice."

"Foxfire left me. These Hines women will do that rather than face rejection."

"I didn't reject her." The lie tastes like ashes in my mouth.

"You did. You brought her into your life, and threw her to the wolves. That's not how you treat a mate. That's not how you raised me."

Ours. My wolf howls. *Our mate.*

I swallow the pain. "She left of her own accord."

"Then get her back," my son snarls. "Lay down your damn pride and protect your mate."

Yes! My wolf agrees.

"—Sir," Tank adds.

"You're a good man, son."

"I'm what you raised me to be."

"Proud of you."

"Dad…" Tank sighs. Whatever he says next is gonna be heavy. "I love you."

I grip the phone tighter. Try to swallow. "I love you, too." We don't say these words aloud. But why not? Life's too damn short to keep everything bottled up.

Tank and I clear our throats simultaneously. He speaks first. "Sunny's here. We'll keep her safe until you come. Just don't take too long."

We say our goodbyes and hang up.

Sunny. Fuck. I have to get her back. Now.

I stride back inside to get my keys and my vest.

"Titus?" Alpha Green calls from the corner. The rest of the council ranges around the room, eating leftover sandwiches. "Can you take the pack bus to the hotel down the road and get the rest of our guests settled?"

"No. I'm leaving."

"What? Is this about the human?" Green's eyes narrow. "Because she left. Pierce saw her take off as he was walking in."

I stop at the door. "You knew she left and didn't tell me?" I snarl at my alpha.

His nostrils flare. "I thought you were getting rid of her." There's warning in his voice, but I don't give a shit.

"You had no right to send her away!" I'm outright

yelling now. The rest of the council members' mouths are hanging open. No one challenges Green this way.

"I didn't send her away. Anyway, she's a human. She doesn't belong among shifters, and she knows that. Better than you it seems. Where are you going?"

I grab my vest off the chair and shrug it on. "To get her back."

"Titus, you can't be with her. I forbid it."

"Fuck that." The words are out of my mouth before I can think.

"Excuse me? What did you say—"

"I'm going after Sunny. She's mine."

"She's human. You're pack. She doesn't belong."

"She's my mate."

"You can't bring a human in here. Not to my pack."

"Then I'm out," I bark.

"What?" Pierce gasps. The room full of shifters quiets. They're all watching—Allison, Fiona, Declan, Laurie, and the rest. The entire council.

Goosebumps dance on my arm. My wolf holds his breath. He knows what I'm about to say can't be rescinded.

"I'm out," I repeat. "Out of the pack."

Alpha Green is almost purple. He doesn't take well to people standing up to him. "You leave here, Titus, you don't come back."

"Sounds good to me." I turn on my heel and head for the door. Not smart to turn your back to an angry wolf— and Green is angry like I've never seen before—but I don't give a fuck. None of the council can take me. I'm too big, too strong.

My rage carries me halfway across the parking lot. When I get to my bike, I slow.

Fuck. I left my pack. Fuck! It's my past all over again. Kicked out because of a woman. But this time is different. Tank was just a little guy, and I had to protect him. Now he's grown. My choices are my own. They affect no one but me.

And Sunny. My wolf reminds me.

Right. Sunny. Nothing matters except getting her back. For the first time in a long time, I'm seeing clearly.

I throw my leg over my bike and rev it into gear. With the sun sinking over my shoulder, I head to Tucson.

No more running. This ends tonight.

CHAPTER 13

 *unny*

"SUNNY?"

"Foxfire, what? It's late," I squint at her silhouette in the hall light. My head throbs in protest.

"Sorry. Someone's here to talk to you."

What? "Who…" I sense the change in the air. A prickle of a familiar presence. Only Titus sets off my senses like this. "No."

"I think you should talk to him. "

"Foxfire," Tank calls. My daughter disappears. I roll off the bed. If I'm going to face him, I'm going to stand on my own two freak. Feet.

Oh who am I kidding? I'm a freak. I'll always be a freak. I set my shoulders. I'm not changing for a man. Not even Titus.

His frame fills the doorway and the room falls away. He's the only thing I see.

"Sunny."

"Titus." On second thought, I'm not going to stand. I sink back gracefully a second before my knees give out. "What do you want?"

"You."

"Funny, that's not what I heard." Yes, this is what it sounds like when a fifty-something-year-old woman acts like a teenager. But I'm entitled to some attitude.

"I know what you heard." He spreads his hands. If he didn't look so damn contrite I would kick him out of the room right now.

"I fucked up. For a minute—for one *stupid* minute—I actually thought my place in the pack was more important than you are. But I was wrong."

To my shock, he drops to his knees in front of me. I must be nuts, because all I can think of is climbing on, straddling his waist the way I did at the waterfall.

Instead, I press my knuckles into my mouth to keep him from seeing the wobble of my chin. It's a failed attempt because some tears fall onto the back of my hand.

"Baby," he says softly. He covers the hand at my mouth with his own and gently pulls it away, stroking the back of it with his thumb. "I hurt you. I'm so sorry. I had my head shoved up my ass. I planned on talking to you after the meeting about our future. Because I love you and I want to be with you. But then when Alpha Green came at me with questions, I panicked. And believe me, I felt the betrayal of those words the moment they came from my mouth. And I told myself it would all be okay, because once I talked to you, I could set Green straight."

Even if I couldn't feel his energy, misery's painted all over his face. I can't doubt his words. Titus has never been a player or liar, anyway.

"But that part's done already, so I'm sure as hell hoping I can convince you to keep me around."

"What part's done already?"

"I quit the pack. Told Green you were my mate and he can shove it because I'm sticking with you."

I gasp. "No… Titus."

Alarm creeps into his gaze.

"The pack means everything to you. I don't want you to give it up for me."

He brushes a lock of hair away from my face. "I don't care about the pack. All I care about is you. Please say you'll have me. I won't slow you down, I promise. We'll have to get a bigger RV, but I'll go with you—wherever your free spirit wants to go."

I give a watery laugh. "Titus, no," I repeat and he looks even more alarmed. "I mean no, we don't have to live in an RV. I wouldn't drag you around the country on the craft circuit."

Titus' brows draw together. "I'm not sure what you're saying, sunshine. Please tell me it's that you'll let me be your mate."

I touch the bite mark. "From what I understand, that's already a done deal."

Guilt washes over Titus' face. "I'm sorry. I should've told you. I just didn't want to scare you. I know how you don't like to settle down."

175

I reach out and touch his face. His silver beard is soft beneath my fingers. "Titus, you have it all wrong. I'd be happy to settle down."

His brows go up. "You would?"

"Yes. With you. Here. Or anywhere. If you're really looking for a mate."

He gives a pained laugh. "I'm not looking for a mate."

I flush. "Oh, I—"

"I already found her."

"You did?" I whisper.

He reaches up to cup my face with both hands. "I did. She's right here in front of me."

"You don't mind that I'm human?" I have to ask. I can't be in this relationship feeling inadequate. I've been there, done that. Not doing it again.

"I fucking love that you're human." He pulls me onto his lap, where I wanted to be all along.

I wrap my arms around his neck. "You do?"

"Hell yes. It means I get to impress you with my massive strength." He flexes his thighs beneath me, making me rise an inch.

I laugh and nip at his lip. "And your tremendous prowess."

His cock gets hard, lifting me some more. "Yes, that."

"And your beautiful silver wolf." I kiss him.

He takes the lead, holding the sides of my face to claim my mouth. "Yes, that, too." His tongue slides against mine, mustache tickles my lips.

"I love you, Sunny Hines."

"I love you, too, wolf-man."

Somehow, he stands up with me still wrapped around his waist.

"Where are we going?" I ask as he carries me out of the guest room.

"To the VW." He lowers his voice to a quiet rumble only I can hear. "I can't fuck you in my son's house. It feels too weird."

I laugh. "I'm sure Foxfire and Tank will both thank you for that."

"I guaran—fucking-tee it," he says. "Especially with how loud I'm gonna make you scream."

"Maybe we'd better drive Daisy a few blocks away, then," I suggest, nipping at his neck.

"A few *miles* away," he agrees.

EPILOGUE

S *unny*

"A TOAST," Foxfire says.

"To what?" Tank sets down the heaping platter on the picnic table. Titus is cleaning the grill, prepping to cook a mountain of meat.

"To love." I grin up at Titus. He's wearing a *May I Suggest the Sausage* apron with an arrow pointing downwards. I bought it for him at a farmer's market and he swore he wouldn't wear it... until I spent a few nights sampling his meat. Foxfire threatened to blind herself when he came out wearing it.

"Love? Too cheesy," Foxfire complains.

"No wonder I don't have grandbabies."

"Sunny!" She glares at me, then at Titus, and averts her eyes to the sky. "Why me? What have I done to deserve this?"

"Stop being so dramatic. Titus and I are adults with healthy, normal libidos—"

"Do not ever mention your libido to me again."

"—and we're meant for each other. We're making up for lost time." After a few days of sneaking away to the VW bus, we finally broke in the bed in Foxfire's guest room last night. I blow a kiss to Titus. "Love you, man-wolf."

"Love you, too, sunshine."

"Oh my goddess, I just threw up a little," Foxfire mutters.

"I'll get the door." Tank stomps off.

I cock my head. "I didn't hear the doorbell ring—"

The doorbell rings.

"Super senses." Foxfire taps her ear. "Speaking of which, how long are you guys gonna shack up here? It's not that I don't love your gluten-free pancakes, Sunny, it's just that with our shifter hearing we can hear you through the walls."

"Oh, I'm sorry, darling, were we talking too loud?"

"It's not the talking that bothers me."

"Ooooooh." I look at Titus and giggle. "Well, you know how these wolves are. So virile and—"

Foxfire slams her hands over her ears and chants, "La la la."

Titus gently pulls her wrist away long enough to tell her, "We're putting an offer on a house tomorrow. Tonight we'll get a hotel."

"Thanks, Mr. T. You don't mind if I call you Mr. T?"

"I mind," Titus deadpans, but winks at me.

Foxfire chuckles. Tank sticks his head through the doorway. "They're here."

"Ahhh," my daughter squeals, and runs to hug a familiar-looking red-headed woman with a splash of brown freckles across her nose. A hulking man hovers between the redhead and Tank. He gives Titus a suspicious look before jerking his chin up in greeting.

Foxfire grabs the woman's hand and drags her over to me. "Sunny, this is Jordy. She's—"

"Johnny's sister," I say. "Oh my dear, he told me about you. You were just a little thing, but you look so like him." I wrap her in a hug.

"Careful," Jordy's bodyguard warns. I loosen my arms and draw back to study Jordy.

"And you must be Grizz," Foxfire greets the big guy. He grunts hello.

"Wait a minute." I narrow my eyes. Jordy's aura is soft and glowing, pulsing with two heartbeats.

"Grandbaby," I shout. "Grandbaby! Titus, we're having grandbabies."

"Well, actually," Foxfire says. "Jordy is my father's sister so that makes her my aunt and her baby your niece…"

"Grandbaby," I coo, hugging Jordy gently. "Oh, I'm so happy for you." I turn and throw my arms open to Grizz. He looks mildly alarmed as I give him a big Sunny hug. "Welcome to the family." I smile up at him.

"Thank you." He pats my back once. I'll get him there.

"Oh, I'm so happy." I wave my hands at my face to dry my tears. "Titus, isn't this wonderful?"

"Sure is, sunshine." Titus pulls me in for a kiss.

"Ewwwww," Tank and Foxfire groan in unison.

"Oh stop it, you two. You're pretty loud yourself. *Big Daddy*." I bug my eyes out at Tank.

Foxfire pretends to retch into a potted plant.

"Beer?" Tank offers Grizz.

"Soda. For both of us." The big guy fusses over his mate, pulling out her seat and making sure she has a cushion.

"I'm fine," she whispers and smiles at him so sweetly I tear up again. When he leans down and kisses her freckled forehead, I have to wipe my eyes.

I lean against Titus and watch them with hearts in my eyes. "I'm so happy, Titus. Are you happy?"

"I've got my sunshine." He wraps an arm around me and keeps grilling. "Of course I am."

THANK you so much for reading the *Bad Boy Alpha* series! It's been a fabulous ride. We have two spin-off series —*Shifter Ops*, featuring the black wolf pack up in Taos, and Midnight Doms.

If you enjoyed this book, we always, always appreciate your reviews and recommendations. It's readers like you who make it possible for indie authors to get their books out to the world. Thank you!

--Come meet Renee and Lee in person at Shameless Con.

ACKNOWLEDGMENTS

Thank you to our beta readers Aubrey Cara, Claire G. and Hayley for their help.

Thank you to the members of Lee's Goddess Group and Renee's Romper Room for your support and love (if you're not a member and you're in Facebook, please join!). Thanks to our ARC readers and to Ardent Prose PR and the bloggers who support our releases. You are all amazing!

WANT MORE? ALPHA'S MOON

PUERTO RICO

Deke

The Puerto Rican jungle is thick and humid. At night, the song of the *coquí* frogs chorus echo all around the stifling darkness. I creep silently over the rotting leaves on the rainforest floor, slinking into position. Channing's already there on his belly, squinting through the sight of his sniper rifle.

"We got two guards on deck," Channing whispers.

With our shifter hearing, we don't need comms units to hear each other. Nor do I need night vision goggles. That's the reason Colonel Johnson created a special ops team composed entirely of shifters. He's one of us. He knew how much we'd be capable of when our abilities didn't have to be hidden from our human counterparts.

A quick glance, and I clearly see the outline of two cartel members standing in front of the shack's open door frame. Each of them hold machine guns.

"What do you think—hostage inside?" Channing murmurs. "Tied, gagged?"

"Gagged. Tied with rope." That's my guess, anyway.

"Don't see any dogs," Channing says. "So we wait for Rafe's signal."

I nod and strip out of my outer clothes, including dog tags. Colonel Johnson had special camo underclothing designed for us. The fabric is stretchy and flexible enough to accommodate both human and wolf form. I guess the army higher ups thought having our ding-dongs hanging out after we shifted back would make us feel vulnerable. Like we give a shit who sees us naked.

I shift, but try to maintain some control, to hold back my wolf. He's antsy to get on with the hunt. The sad truth is that after years of war conditioning, he's always ready for the kill, especially when there's a civilian rescue involved. The need to protect sometimes overwhelms reason.

The signal is a long blast on a dog whistle, a sound no human can hear. When it comes, Channing and I dart forward. As a wolf, I'm faster, and I race ahead.

We're almost there when I pick up a rumbling sound up the road. Trouble coming in the form of an old diesel truck. Fuck! More kidnappers showing up to help stand guard.

My ears prick at the ear splitting sound of the dog whistle. Two short blasts this time—Rafe telling us to get out.

I try to turn back. To follow orders. The part of me that still knows chain of command fights for control.

But my wolf isn't having it.

It's too late—I smell the package. The frightened human who's perhaps given up on being rescued.

It's wrong to disobey a command. We may not be Special Ops any more, but wolves also follow their leader, and Rafe is our alpha. Still, I can't stop my wolf. He needs to save the human. I bound forward, paws eating up ground as I head toward the shack.

"Abort mission," Channing growls, but I'm too far gone. I leap, a silent shadow, onto the wooden platform.

The first guard dies almost silently. His body thumps to the deck. The other guard whirls, fingers scrambling for the trigger of his machine gun when two hundred plus pounds of wolf lands on him. He goes down, and I silence him with my teeth.

Permanently.

I hear shots and raise my head. My muzzle is slick, and there's blood in my mouth. On the other side of the shack, our team attacks the diesel truck. I forced them into this by not following orders. It's the only option now.

A few more shots, a growl from Lance's wolf, and the sound of screams drowns out the chorus of *coquí* frogs for a moment. Then the truck engine cuts off, and there's silence.

"Goddammit, Deke!" Channing whisper-shouts. He's still in human form, slinking up to the deck with his rifle outstretched. "You were supposed to follow orders."

My wolf bares his teeth at him.

"Fucking *loco*," Channing mutters as he brushes by me. He follows proper protocol, casing each dark corner before entering the shack. A few seconds later, he starts talking in a low, soothing voice to the hostage.

I'm glad he can because I would scare the hell out of her.

I growl and turn away, my nose to the ground, making sure all threats have been eliminated.

Gangsters: dead. Hostage: rescued. Mission accomplished. The only problem? The action was over in less than ninety seconds. My wolf wants more.

I lope off the deck and around the shack to the diesel truck. There's blood spattered on the cab and two gang members dead—one in the front seat, one a few feet from the passenger door.

Lance stands nearby, disassembling the target's semi-automatics. He's in his camo underclothing from shifting. His dog tags glint on his bare chest—he didn't have time to remove them before shifting.

"Fuck, Deke," he greets me. "I ruined a good pair of khakis for you." He wrenches the metal gun pieces apart and drops them into an open bag at his feet.

I make myself useful, loping back up the hill to Lance's stakeout spot to retrieve his pack. We keep an extra change of clothes for this contingency. Lance hadn't expected to shift, but to finish the mission, my wolf's defiance forced him to. My pack brothers always have my back no matter what.

"Thanks," Lance grunts when I return. He dresses quickly.

"Let's move out. Channing's already gone with the package." The *package* being the hostage. The one we, as mercenaries, were just paid a sizable amount of money to retrieve for someone high up in our government who didn't want to risk an active military team on this job. "Rendezvous at HQ."

A crackle in the brush behind me announces the arrival of my alpha.

"What the hell was that, soldier?" Rafe growls at me even though we're no longer technically soldiers.

I duck my head in contrition.

"I think it went well, Sarge," Lance says mildly before tugging on his shirt.

"No one fucking asked you." Rafe points up the hill. "Move out, now."

Lance shrugs on his pack and obeys.

Rafe points to me. "We're going to talk about this," he promises.

Four hours later, we're back at HQ, an empty airplane hanger. Soon a tiny charter plane will show up to secret us back home. Lance helped me hose off the blood—my wolf was reluctant to remove all traces of its kills. I went for a run first, trying to rid myself of the pent-up energy, waiting until the last possible minute to shift.

Channing arrives at HQ last and doesn't bother with the hose. He sticks his head in a bucket of water and then uses a rag to wipe off his face paint. "The package was delivered safely," he announces. "All's well that ends well."

"Not so fucking fast." Rafe marches back into the hanger from the outside, where he was taking a call from command. "We've got a problem." My alpha rounds on me and points. "Your wolf is out of control, Deke." He's not wrong. I disobeyed a direct order.

"Yes, Sergeant." My voice is gravely, guttural, as if my

throat is unused to human words. We still call Rafe Sarge even though we're no longer in the Army.

"Did you have orders to kill, Deke?"

A sick feeling roils in my belly. This is why Rafe decided we needed to get out of the service last year. Every hunt, I was becoming more feral. We all were. Rafe said we had to leave before we all lost our humanity and needed to be put down.

"In Deke's defense, he only killed the Tangos," Channing offers.

Rafe bares his teeth at Channing, who ducks his head and puts up his hands in surrender.

"We didn't have kill orders," Rafe growls.

"Colonel Johnson wouldn't contract us if he didn't expect a body count," Lance counters.

"That's only because Deke's out of control," Rafe shouts.

The weight on my chest increases.

Fuck.

Rafe paces, his boots striking the concrete floor in a staccato beat. Rafe can glide silently if he wants to. He's making noise now to make a point. I brace myself for it.

It comes all too soon. Rafe stops in front of me and blows on the dog whistle. I stand at attention, fighting not to cringe at the high pitched sound. Channing and Lance snap their hands over their ears.

"What does that mean, soldier?" Rafe barks at me.

"All systems go, sir!" I shout back.

Rafe blows the dog whistle again, two short blasts. "And that?"

"Abort mission, sir!"

Rafe gets right in my face, yellow eyes fixed on mine. I stare off in the distance, fighting my wolf's restless urge to break position and attack.

This is a test. If I break position and challenge my alpha, it's a sign I'm way too far gone. Something my pack has been worried about for a couple years now.

I have to pass this test.

I force myself to think of puppies. Innocent toddlers. Human females—that's a new thought, but for some reason it comes to mind. Like I might reward myself for passing this test by seeking out pleasure.

As if.

My team won't let me near humans. Not after that bar fight last year. My wolf is way too aggressive and unpredictable. Too bloodthirsty.

But the thought of fragile creatures is enough. My wolf relaxes.

My alpha stands inches away. He senses the change in my body and nods. But he doesn't let me off the hook.

"Discipline, soldier," Rafe growls right in my ringing ear. "It's all that stands between us and moon madness."

I unclench my jaw. "Yes, sir."

READ NOW

READ ALL THE BAD BOY ALPHA
BOOKS

Bad Boy Alphas Series
Alpha's Temptation
Alpha's Danger
Alpha's Prize
Alpha's Challenge
Alpha's Obsession
Alpha's Desire
Alpha's War
Alpha's Mission
Alpha's Bane
Alpha's Secret
Alpha's Prey
Alpha's Blood
Alpha's Sun

Shifter Ops
Alpha's Moon
Alpha's Vow
Alpha's Revenge

Midnight Doms

Alpha's Blood
His Captive Mortal
Additional books by other authors

WANT FREE BOOKS?

-Go to http://subscribepage.com/alphastemp to sign up for Renee Rose's newsletter and receive a free copy of *Alpha's Temptation, Theirs to Protect, Owned by the Marine, Theirs to Punish, The Alpha's Punishment, Disobedience at the Dressmaker's* and *Her Billionaire Boss*. In addition to the free stories, you will also get special pricing, exclusive previews and news of new releases.

-Go to www.leesavino.com to sign up for Lee Savino's awesomesauce mailing list and get a FREE Berserker book —too hot to publish anywhere else!

OTHER TITLES BY RENEE ROSE

Paranormal

Bad Boy Alphas Series

Alpha's Temptation

Alpha's Danger

Alpha's Prize

Alpha's Challenge

Alpha's Obsession

Alpha's Desire

Alpha's War

Alpha's Mission

Alpha's Bane

Alpha's Secret

Alpha's Prey

Alpha's Sun

Shifter Ops

Alpha's Moon

Alpha's Vow

Alpha's Revenge

Wolf Ranch Series

Rough

Wild

Feral

Savage

Fierce

Ruthless

Untamed

Wolf Ridge High Series

Alpha Bully

Alpha Knight

Midnight Doms

Alpha's Blood

His Captive Mortal

Alpha Doms Series

The Alpha's Hunger

The Alpha's Promise

The Alpha's Punishment

Other Paranormal

The Winter Storm: An Ever After Chronicle

Contemporary

Chicago Bratva

"Prelude" in Black Light: Roulette War

The Director

The Fixer

"Owned" in Black Light: Roulette Rematch

The Enforcer

Vegas Underground Mafia Romance

King of Diamonds

Mafia Daddy

Jack of Spades

Ace of Hearts

Joker's Wild

His Queen of Clubs

Dead Man's Hand

Wild Card

Daddy Rules Series

Fire Daddy

Hollywood Daddy

Stepbrother Daddy

Master Me Series

Her Royal Master

Her Russian Master

Her Marine Master

Yes, Doctor

Zandian Pet

Their Zandian Mate

His Human Possession

Zandian Brides

Night of the Zandians

Bought by the Zandians

Mastered by the Zandians

Zandian Lights

Kept by the Zandian

Claimed by the Zandian

Stolen by the Zandian

Other Sci-Fi

The Hand of Vengeance

Her Alien Masters

Regency

The Darlington Incident

Humbled

The Reddington Scandal

The Westerfield Affair

Pleasing the Colonel

Western

His Little Lapis

The Devil of Whiskey Row

The Outlaw's Bride

Medieval

Mercenary

Medieval Discipline

Lords and Ladies

The Knight's Prisoner

Betrothed

The Knight's Seduction

The Conquered Brides (5 book box set)

Held for Ransom (out of print)

Renaissance

Renaissance Discipline

Paranormal romance

The Berserker Saga and Berserker Brides (menage werewolves)

These fierce warriors will stop at nothing to claim their mates.

Draekons (Dragons in Exile) with Lili Zander (menage alien dragons)

Crashed spaceship. Prison planet. Two big, hulking, bronzed aliens who turn into dragons. The best part? The dragons insist I'm their mate.

Bad Boy Alphas with Renee Rose (bad boy werewolves)

Never ever date a werewolf.

Tsenturion Masters with Golden Angel

Who knew my e-reader was a portal to another galaxy? Now I'm stuck with a fierce alien commander who wants to claim me as his own.

Contemporary Romance

Royal Bad Boy

I'm not falling in love with my arrogant, annoying, sex god boss. Nope. No way.

Royally Fake Fiancé

The Duke of New Arcadia has an image problem only a fiancé can fix. And I'm the lucky lady he's chosen to play Cinderella.

Beauty & The Lumberjacks

After this logging season, I'm giving up sex. For...reasons.

Her Marine Daddy

My hot Marine hero wants me to call him daddy...

Her Dueling Daddies

Two daddies are better than one.

Innocence: dark mafia romance with Stasia Black

I'm the king of the criminal underworld. I always get what I want. And she is my obsession.

Beauty's Beast: a dark romance with Stasia Black

Years ago, Daphne's father stole from me. Now it's time for her to pay her family's debt...with her body.

ABOUT RENEE ROSE

USA TODAY BESTSELLING AUTHOR RENEE ROSE loves a dominant, dirty-talking alpha hero! She's sold over a million copies of steamy romance with varying levels of kink. Her books have been featured in USA Today's *Happily Ever After* and *Popsugar*. Named Eroticon USA's Next Top Erotic Author in 2013, she has also won *Spunky and Sassy's* Favorite Sci-Fi and Anthology author, *The Romance Reviews* Best Historical Romance, and *has* hit the *USA Today* list seven times with her Wolf Ranch series and various anthologies.

Please follow her on:
   Bookbub | Goodreads

Renee loves to connect with readers!
www.reneeroseromance.com
reneeroseauthor@gmail.com

ABOUT LEE SAVINO

Lee Savino is a USA today bestselling author, mom and chocoholic.

Warning: Do not read her Berserker series, or you will be addicted to the huge, dominant warriors who will stop at nothing to claim their mates.

I repeat: Do. Not. Read. The Berserker Saga. Particularly not the thrilling excerpt below.

Download a free book from www.leesavino.com (don't read that either. Too much hot, sexy lovin').